Dear David,
Happy Reading!
Nick Colom

HELL OF A MESS

PRAISE FOR
Love & Bullets
a series by Nick Kolakowski

"Nick Kolakowski takes us on another incredibly visceral and vivacious ride among the lowlife and the lovers that populate his unique imagination. Love and Bullets is vintage Nick . Funny , fast paced and just tinged with just enough darkness to make you afraid for his characters. Not to be missed!"

—**S.A. Cosby** NYT's bestselling author of *Razorblade Tears*

"Ruthless, off-the-wall and surprisingly heartfelt, A Brutal Bunch of Heartbroken Saps is much more than a heist book, and showcases the skills of an emerging writer in Nick Kolakowski. Saps is the kind of book you read fast and revisit immediately to savor the experience again."

—**Alex Segura**, bestselling author of *Secret Identity*

"Dark, bleak and in-your-face, take-no-prisoners prose, everything you want in crime fiction."

—**Frank Bill**, author of *Donnybrook*

"A Brutal Bunch of Heartbroken Saps is a hell of a yarn that sets the stage for what should be an essential series for fans of the genre."

—*Angel Luis Colón*, author of *No Happy Endings*

"A Brutal Bunch of Heartbroken Saps is a hell of a ride. Whatever the outcome, Kolakowski's fabulous writing shines and the twists and turns will keep you reading to the very last page. A wonderful, entertaining read."

—**Jen Conley**, author of *Seven Ways to Get Rid of Harry*

"It's no surprise that Nick Kolakowski brought the heat with his latest novel. His stripped-down, hard-boiled prose, the explosive dialogue, or the wickedly insane and diabolical humor. Grab hold of this one with both hands and hold on tight."

—**Eryk Pruitt**, author of *What We Reckon*

More titles by Nick Kolakowski

(Shotgun Honey Books)

A Brutal Bunch of Heartbroken Saps
Slaugherhouse Blues
Main Bad Guy
Love & Bullets: Megabomb Edition
Payback is Forever

(Down & Out Books)

Boise Long Pig Club
Rattlesnake Rodeo
Maxine Unleashes Doomsday

(Other releases)

Absolute Unit
Lockdown:
Stories of Crime, Terror, and Hope During a Pandemic

A LOVE & BULLETS HOOKUP
BOOK FOUR

HELL OF A MESS

NICK KOLAKOWSKI

SHOTGUN HONEY

2022

Published by Shotgun Honey Books

215 Loma Road
Charleston, WV 25314
www.ShotgunHoney.com

Cover by Bad Fido.

First Printing 2022.

ISBN-10: 1-956957-14-6
ISBN-13: 978-1-956957-14-3

9 8 7 6 5 4 3 2 1   22 21 20 19 18 17

To the folks on the 'cord...
dirty deeds explained dirt cheap.

1

IT WAS THE worst possible timing—or maybe the best. A major hurricane churning its way up the East Coast, unleashing chaos: traffic jams, stripped store shelves, canceled flights, subways and trains shut down. Overloaded 911. Distracted cops. Prime opportunity for crime—if Fiona could dodge floods and flying debris. Boz offering her a new life for two hours' work made it worth the risk.

Raindrops pattered the windshield of the junky Toyota SUV. The rainbands arriving faster now, only twenty minutes apart, as the hurricane's fingers scratched New Jersey and the southern edge of New York. On the radio, a breathless announcer warned the storm was the biggest in decades, almost Biblical—everyone in low-lying areas needed to evacuate to higher ground or kiss their ass goodbye.

Fireball, dark and small-boned in a way that reminded Fiona of a crow, leaned back in the passenger seat so he could place his ratty sneakers on the dashboard. "I swear, you'd think nobody's lived through a hurricane before," he said. "I'm in the supermarket two days ago, the shelves are already stripped bare, it's total panic. This Asian guy walks up and puts his hand on this six-pack of beer, and I tell him, 'Do you know kung fu or something?'"

"Get your feet off the dash," Fiona said, staring through the windshield at the luxury condo across the avenue, its lobby doors blurred by curtains of rain and dancing litter.

"Soon as I say that, the guy starts freaking out. He's yelling, 'What, I look Asian so I gotta know kung fu?'" Fireball snorted. "And I say, 'No, you jerk, you *better* know kung fu, because that's the last six-pack and I was already reaching for it.'"

"Let me guess," Fiona said, smacking his feet off the dashboard with the back of her hand. "You totally kicked his ass?"

"No, it turned out he was some kind of martial-arts master." Fireball kicked the air. "Slammed me to the ground—*pow!*—took the six-pack. It's amazing how violent people can get when they're frightened..."

"I wasn't serious about you beating him," she said, her gaze shifting to the rearview mirror. Nobody visible on the narrow street behind them, the wet cobblestones reflecting the scuttling gray sky. Under normal circumstances, she loved this border between Tribeca and Battery Park City, where old brick and ironwork gave way to Lower Manhattan's glass spires. Now she couldn't stop thinking about an interactive map she saw on a news website a few days ago, the one showing how seven or eight feet of storm surge would put this area underwater.

"I can fight," Fireball said. "I can kick an unholy amounts of ass."

"Sure, in a video game," she said. "Now focus. It's almost time."

"Already?" Groaning in mock exhaustion, Fireball made a big show of pushing his sleeve back to check his cheap digital watch. "You're sure he's that exact? Because..."

Her phone beeped. She answered it in her most cheerful voice, just in case Boz's Inside Man was calling on speaker: "Wok the Line. May I take your order?"

"Yeah, this is two-oh-five Warren, penthouse. You know our usual order, ah, we might not..." Boz's Inside Man paused. More chatter in the background now, loud with anger or excitement.

"Hello?" If something was up, this was the best time for her to abort. Go home and ride out watery Armageddon with a bottle of wine and a joint, listen to Bill discuss his latest insane plan for a heist.

"No, come up," the Inside Man said, and sighed. "But just bring the usual order, okay? Just the usual order, got that? Nothing extra."

"You got it. Ten minutes." Ending the call, she slipped the phone into the left-rear pocket of her jeans. "Something's up."

"Huh?"

"The guy sounded weird. Like he was having second thoughts."

"But he said come up?"

"Yeah. With the usual order. He kept saying it. 'Usual order, usual order.'" She wondered whether the actual restaurant would call the penthouse when nobody phoned for dinner at the regular time. Probably not. Whoever handled the phone at the real Wok the Line hopefully assumed their favorite customer wasn't psychopathic enough to order a delivery person into an oncoming category 4 storm.

"Maybe he was trying to tell you to call it off."

"Maybe. But I'm going up anyway. Just to see."

"You think that's wise?"

"You want to tell Boz we chickened out?"

"I guess not."

"Besides, I'm doing the hard part."

"Okay, okay, whatever." Fireball rolled his eyes. "Let's get this done before Noah's Ark sails by." From the waterproof backpack in the footwell, he pulled out a battered laptop and opened it, waking the machine. He clicked, summoning a black window with a command prompt, and hammered the keyboard. "You can see how the building's whole wireless setup is outdated, which is nineteen fantastic flavors of excellent," he said, as if she could understand anything about the lines of code unspooling from the prompt. "You want all the cameras looped?"

"Yeah, I guess. Work faster." She imagined a wall of water churning up the street behind her, flipping cars and shattering storefronts. Hurricane wind pushed against the windows like a giant's hand, rocking the hatchback gently on its springs.

"Okay, okay, okay," he said, smacking two keys with a theatrical flourish. "Cameras are primed."

Onscreen, a new window popped up, revealing a grid of camera views: angles on a lobby, stairwells, a parking garage lined with expensive automobiles. "Still no cameras on the penthouse level?" she asked.

"Nah. Readout says they're disabled."

"And you have no idea where that server is."

"Actually, I do, but I've been opting not to tell you. Just for my own sick amusement."

"Don't screw with me."

"No, I have no idea where it is. We just gotta take Boz's word it exists."

"Unfortunately." She drew her pistol and pushed the slide back a quarter-inch so she could verify the round in the chamber. Leaning forward, she pushed up her left cuff and slipped the weapon into the plastic holster strapped to her ankle. She patted the compact taser in the inner pocket of her jacket, along with the five riot cuffs and the USB stick tucked in the right hip pocket of her jeans. It felt weird to wear all this equipment again after so long, but she might need all of it. Why had the Inside Man hesitated on the phone?

"Whole building's got those dumbass smart locks, which are now officially my bitch," he said. "How many guys up there?"

"Two security dudes, but our inside guy's one of them." She slipped a wireless earbud into her left ear. "Owner's away, Boz said."

"Who owns it?"

"Boz didn't tell me. For my own good, he said. Did some research when I looked up the floor plan, it said some LLC. No news stories about a recent sale, so it wasn't a famous actor or CEO." She snapped her fingers. "Give me the bag."

From the footwell, Fireball hoisted a white plastic bag stacked with takeout containers. The bag featured the logo of a red rooster above *Wok the Line 212-555-2124* in slashing blue script. Fiona slipped it into her lap, surprised at its heat more than an hour after they picked it up from the restaurant. She took a deep, comforting sniff of fried chicken and fragrant rice before flipping her hood over her head and adjusting her mask over her nose and mouth. A worldwide pandemic and its variants, despite the horrors, had one key benefit: you could hide your face in public and nobody thought twice about it.

"See you in the funny papers," she said, and pushed open her door. It took real effort. The wind screamed through the widening gap and cold rain needled her forehead. She almost slipped on the slick sidewalk as she climbed out and slammed the door. Maybe an inch of water shimmered on the street—not a danger yet.

Over the storm's rising roar, she heard Fireball yell, "What the hell are funny papers?"

Nobody visible on the street. Hunched over the plastic bag, she scuttled for the front doors. She estimated twenty-five minutes for this op, in and out, hopefully no killing, just a little electrocution if necessary. Unless the situation collapsed into a goat rodeo, she only intended to use the pistol for persuasion. She was trying to turn over a new and more peaceful leaf these days.

The lobby was a marble box with a massive slab of a reception desk blocking the way to the elevator banks. Two receptionists in blue suits sat at the desk, their faces carefully blank as she shoved through the revolving door. They looked like football players who had to find another line of work after too many injuries on the field. Based on their respective hair styles, she decided to call them Dreadlocks and Baldie.

"Hey," she said, lifting the bag. "I got a delivery. Penthouse."

"Okay." Dreadlocks picked up a phone and dialed.

"Pretty wet out there," Baldie said, his eyes flicking over her.

"That's what happens with hurricanes." Did he believe her delivery-drone outfit? Every evening at five, someone wearing one of these bright red jackets ('Wok the Line' on the back in huge font, above the rooster logo) delivered the same meal to the penthouse. She should have been invisible to these guys.

Phone jammed to his ear, Dreadlocks frowned. What was taking so long?

"I bet you're cute under all that gear," Baldie said, smiling at her. "What's your name?"

"June," she said.

Dreadlocks spoke a few words into the phone and looked up. "You're cleared," he told Fiona.

"Thanks." She walked across the lobby, angling toward the elevators beyond the desk. "Back down in a blink."

"Guy up there said he ordered five minutes ago," Dreadlocks said, lowering the phone into its cradle.

"I guess. I just do deliveries." She was almost to the desk, moving fast.

"Pretty quick in weather like this."

She shrugged, already rehearsing her next moves in her mind. Up to the penthouse. Meet the Inside Man. Disable the other bodyguard. Find the server, stick the USB stick into the right slot, squish any trouble until all the information downloaded, and—

Baldie stood, straightening his tie. "I'll escort you up to the penthouse."

"No, I'm all good," she said. "I've been here before."

"No, no, it'd be my pleasure," Baldie said, slipping from behind the desk. He was almost seven feet tall, more than two hundred pounds of pure muscle, and no doubt hired by a place like this because he had security work in his background, cop or military, potential trouble either way. If something weird happened up there, he could use the microphone clipped to his lapel to talk to Dreadlocks, who would call for backup. And these guys had serious private security on speed dial.

The best time to abort this mission would have been in the car. The second-best time was right now. But if she ejected, Boz wouldn't give her what she needed.

She could improvise, right?

She stopped in the elevator bank, Baldie standing too close behind her. As he smacked the 'up' button, he said, "You been delivering long?"

How desperate was this walking pituitary accident? Between her bulky restaurant jacket with its hood, her mask, and her loose pants and combat boots, he couldn't see anything but her eyes and a few wisps of hair. He was one of those jerks who figured if he asked random women often enough, he'd score a quickie in a closet. He totally deserved a hard punch to the throat.

"About a year," she offered, keeping her eyes locked on the digital indicator counting down the floors.

"What you do for fun?" he asked, looming over her now.

"Hang out with my boyfriend," she said.

"Yeah? Your boyfriend lets you go out on a night like this?"

"Sure," she said. "He lets me tie my own shoes, too."

The elevator doors whooshed open, and she stepped inside. The tight confines and wooden paneling reminded her a little too much of a coffin. Baldie followed, hitting the button for the penthouse. The doors hissed shut.

"You don't have to be rude about it," he said. "I'm just talking."

"And I'm just delivering food." Her thumb hooked into her pocket, skimming the edge of the taser.

"Whatever." He shifted away from her.

The lights flickered, the elevator's smooth ascent stuttering.

Please don't lose power, she begged the universe. If I'm stuck in here, I'll kill this guy within twenty minutes, tops.

For once, the universe listened to her. The elevator arrived at the penthouse with a cheerful ping, and the doors opened onto a marble hallway bathed softly by recessed lighting. Oversized canvases hung on the eggshell-white walls, abstract splashes of blue and black and red that cost more than a mansion.

Five big dudes stood in front of the door to their left. They wore gray suits loosely tailored, in the way of bodyguards who wanted to hide their holsters. Their stances said they could take care of themselves in a real fight.

Their presence rendered all her intel some prime A-1 horseshit. What crack-smoking, smooth-brained moron had told Boz there were only two bodyguards up here? How was she going to handle all these guys? Was there a whole platoon inside the apartment, too?

She hesitated in the elevator doorway. Don't freeze, she told herself. Think your way through this. Start with the Inside Man. Which one was he? She should have asked Boz for a photo or a description before heading up here. Another op failure. She was so rusty at this. Stupid, stupid, stupid.

"It's your floor, lady," said Baldie behind her, spitting out the last word like it was poison.

This high up, the building creaked as the winds pummeled it. Working her sweaty grip on the handle of the takeout bag, she stepped into the hallway, ready for anything.

2

CONFRONTED WITH AN epic natural disaster, most people would load up on survival supplies: batteries and flashlights, gallons of distilled water, first aid kits, hand sanitizer and wet wipes, multitools and multipurpose bags, a couple hundred bucks in twenties, dust masks and glow sticks. They would stuff those supplies into a backpack beside the front door and hope they never had to flee for their lives.

Bill was not most people.

As the tropical storm in the Atlantic coalesced into the hurricane bearing down on New York City, he had opted to stock the kitchen and pantry of their borrowed townhouse with cases of wine and cigars, baguettes and prosciutto and jamón ibérico, prime cuts of raw salmon, cute glass jars of roe, and—this was the *pièce de resistance*—a bottle of 1995 Krug Clos du Mesnil Blanc de Blancs Brut. Even if they lost power for a week or more, they had plenty of protein and alcohol, and what more did anyone need, frankly? It wasn't as if he paid for any of it.

Standing at the kitchen counter, he helped himself to a full glass of wine and a thick wad of prosciutto. The wind hummed against the windows, paired with the backbeat of rain.

He was worried about Fiona.

Why had she taken the job? Sure, his idea for a score was complicated, and they would need to wait until well after the storm passed—but it was doable, with the tantalizing possibility of millions at the end of it.

But Fiona was impatient, as usual.

Don't worry, sweetie, she'd told him on the way out the door. *Anything goes wrong, I got the gun!*

What about not killing? he'd retorted—because she was trying to become more Zen, right? Kinder and gentler and all that other crap?

I'll just shoot them in the kneecap! she said before the door slammed behind her.

His wife had a funny concept of Zen.

At least she had Fireball on this delightful caper. That guy was crazy as an outhouse rat, but he was a wizard when it came to cracking passwords and slipping into databases. He had found this cute house for them, in fact, scanning the emails and texts of rich marks until he stumbled onto a hedge fund manager who was out of town for the next five months. The manager might have graduated from Harvard (as he reminded everyone in almost every message), but he was dumb enough to include the front door's unlock code in a text to his lawyer.

Even better, Mister Big Money Guru had left a fancy black titanium credit card in a bedroom drawer. Would he notice enough food charges to restock a high-end restaurant? If the prospect made Bill nervous, hey, what was life without a little uncertainty?

"Fuck 'em if they can't take a joke," Bill muttered as he checked his phone for the fiftieth time in the past hour. No new messages or emails or missed calls. He flicked to his weather app, the screen filling with a big red sawblade chewing up the New Jersey coast. The wreckage of Atlantic City was halfway to Europe at this point. As someone who had once taken a couple hard punches to the kidneys in the bathroom of that fabled metropolis's shadiest casino, he considered such destruction no great loss.

Damn, why hadn't he volunteered to go along with Fiona?

The answer, of course, was simple: She was the bigger badass. While he had engaged in his share of fisticuffs, he would never match Fiona's skill at annihilating bad dudes. In any tense situation, he would likely become a bullet magnet.

Still, he would rather tag along with her. You never knew when you needed a conman who was slick at cards and talking his way through security.

Wine glass in one hand, phone in the other, he stepped around the counter separating the rustic kitchen from the living room, which was decorated like a Russian Tsar's hunting lodge: bear pelts on the hardwood floor, elk and deer heads on the rough white walls, furniture so lacquered he could see his reflection in it. It could have been the 19th century if not for the enormous television screen facing the leather couch. At the room's furthest edge, a narrow flight of stairs descended to a steel door opening onto 23rd Street.

A doorway to his left led to the dim bedroom, which featured more pelts and expensive wood and a four-poster bed large enough to fit a conquering horde. He flicked on the light and stepped inside. The earnest part of him—and yes, it existed—was pleased at the framed photographs on the walls: gaggles of children and dogs tumbling down endless lawns. The kids seemed so happy, and why not? They were a couple decades away from life delivering its punches—death, disease, car payments.

Would he make a good father?

Pros: He would finally have someone to impart all his life's lessons upon, including how to pick a pocket in a Times Square crowd without getting beaten to a bloody pulp. If you could pull off a small-time hustle, you could literally do anything in life.

Cons: Would Bill's lifetime of questionable decisions—combined with some less-than-stellar genes—screw over Bill Junior before he reached adulthood? All kids deserved to start off with a clean slate.

No, having a family would mean giving up their fabulous criminal lifestyle. A clean break. Fiona had told him that before, and she was right. After this North Brother caper, he would hang up his championship belt and retire for good.

His phone beeped. His brand-new smartwatch buzzed, and he tilted his wrist to check the tiny screen and its flashing message:

Boat secured. Maybe after the storm's over, yeah?

He tapped the little microphone icon beside the message, said, "Where are you now?"

Another moment, another message: *Riding out this bad boy in the Newtown Creek YEEE-HAW.*

Well, provided the boat didn't sink, his little island heist was coming together nicely. He returned to the kitchen, where a beautiful leather folder on the counter held his prep materials. If this was indeed his last job, it would be one for the ages.

3

ONE OF THE bodyguards stepped forward, adjusting his lapels. He was older, with a gray crewcut and the thick chest of a lifetime bodybuilder. "Ah, you're here," he said, his voice familiar from the phone: Boz's Inside Man.

"Your order?" she said, flicking her eyes to the extra men, trying to be subtle about it. Was this a double cross of some sort?

"Yeah, that's right." Reaching into his pants pocket, he extracted a wad of bills thick enough to choke a wolf and peeled off three twenties. "Big tip, huh? Thanks for coming out in this weather. Get home safe."

His gaze told her to march back into the elevator and get her ass out of here. Whatever his deal with Boz, things had changed, and the extra security had something to do with it.

The third-best time to abort this mission was right now. Boz's favors wouldn't do her any good if she tried something, failed, and they tossed her body in the Hudson. Her heart-beat thumped loud in her ears, her breath a little ragged—not from fear, she realized, but excitement. She missed the action, didn't she? When you did evil deeds for a living, you never suffered through a boring day.

An idea popped to mind, fully formed. Like a message from her old life, telling her she still had what it took, maybe.

"I need to use the bathroom," she said.

"You can use the one downstairs," Baldie announced behind her.

"No, my bladder's about to explode." She shifted from foot to foot, locking gazes with the Inside Man, trying to deliver a message with just her eyes: *Get me in there and I'll figure it out.*

Another bodyguard stepped beside the Inside Man, reaching for the bag. "C'mon, dude, I'm hungry…"

"Look," she said, injecting a bit of panic. "In fifteen seconds, I'm going to mess up your very expensive carpet with a gallon of piss, okay? And I'll be quick, okay? Nothing's open out there…"

The Inside Man squinted like he was juggling all possible outcomes. How much was Boz paying him? Was it enough to override his hesitation?

The other bodyguard pried the bag from her hand. "Dude, just let her use the front one, okay?"

"You know how Mister Beau feels about that," yet another bodyguard, a human tank with a scar across his face, muttered from beside the door.

The Inside Man straightened. She noted how the other bodyguards kept flicking their eyes to him. He was in charge here. That should make it easy, right? She wanted to scream. Time was ticking and the rain was pouring down, the flood waters rising—

"Fine," the Inside Man said. "We'll escort you in, you do your business, you get the hell out before the Big Boss sees you. Do you understand?"

"Yes." She raised her eyebrows slightly in thanks. Turning to the elevator, she told Baldie, "You can go down now."

"I'll wait here," Baldie said, crossing his arms over his chest. As if nervous around this quality of hired muscle. Or maybe something about the penthouse disturbed him.

"He's trying to get in my pants," she told the bodyguards, and noted with pleasure how Baldie's cheeks reddened as he stepped into the elevator and smacked the button for the lobby. The elevator doors slid shut.

"Come on," the scarred bodyguard said, waving her forward. "We're going to search you before you go in. Don't argue."

Shit. If they patted her down and found the gun and the riot cuffs and the USB stick, it was game over. What kind of delivery person packed such a huge arsenal, even in New York?

"You're not fucking touching me," she snapped at him. "I have a taser in my jacket. I give it to you, I want it back when I leave. Don't argue."

The scarred bodyguard cracked his knuckles. "You're getting searched, hear?"

"Oh, come on, it's the usual girl," whined another bodyguard. "She's not a threat, and I'm friggin' starving."

The usual girl? How could they tell? Nobody had asked her to pull down her mask or hood. What kind of sorry-ass security firm was this, 1-800-ARMED-IDIOTS?

The scarred bodyguard squeezed his lips into a bloodless line as he considered her. "Fine," he said, stepping aside so he could push open the penthouse door. "But if you try shit, you'll get shit on, understand?"

"How poetic." She drew the taser and slapped it into his palm as she entered the penthouse, the Inside Man and the bodyguard with the food on her heels. The heavy door had one of those smart locks Fireball mentioned, a steel box with a flat handle above a small red bulb. No keyhole.

The door slammed behind them. The foyer was the masterpiece of a decorator with an unlimited credit card and an affinity for royal trimmings, from the enormous crystal chandelier to the black marble floor reflecting her as a shimmering ghost. Beyond the foyer, a long hallway led to a great room, its windows aflicker with lightning. Thunder boomed like distant artillery.

"In there," the Inside Man said, gesturing to the right, where the foyer wall was broken by the outline of a door, a discrete golden knob at its center. She pulled it open, revealing a closet-sized bathroom.

The other bodyguard marched down the hallway, swinging the bag of food. When he disappeared around a corner, she whispered to the Inside Man, "What the hell is going on here?"

"Tell Boz," the Inside Man hissed. "Not tonight. Things have changed."

"What changed?"

"Not for you to know, whoever you are."

"Then why'd you order the food?"

"I wanted you to stand down, but the guys were listening. I thought you'd pick up on it."

"Well, I really do need to piss." She entered the bathroom and shut the door behind her. Flicked the lock. It smelled like a rain forest in here. A soft whisper as the Japanese toilet, sensing her presence, automatically raised its lid.

The toilet was ridiculous, and it must have cost a fortune.

If she had a fortune, she would have bought one just like it, because what's the point of money if you can't have a robot blow-dry your ass three times a day?

But she didn't have a fortune. She didn't even have the money for things she needed right now.

She pulled out her phone, praying for signal. One bar. Magnificent.

She texted Fireball: *Lock penthouse front door.*

He texted back: *30 secs.*

She sat on the toilet, grinning as she noted its little control panel with buttons for hot- and cold-water jets, a directed blast of warm air, everything you needed to maintain a hygienic poop chute. She took a deep breath, held it, and slipped the gun from her ankle holster. Recalled the floor plans she found on a luxury real-estate website. The foyer opened onto a hallway opened onto the great room, library to the left and living room to the right. The living room led to the dining room, followed by the kitchen. If she went through the library, a left turn would place her in a hallway branching into four bedrooms, complete with bathrooms and walk-in closets. Most of the rooms opened onto the penthouse's wraparound terrace.

The gazillion-dollar question: Where had the owner tucked the servers amidst all this ultra-expensive square footage?

On their drive through Manhattan, Fireball guessed one of the bedrooms had been converted to an office. *If there's any kind of server, it'll be in there*, he told her. *And whatever data it holds, it's too dangerous to store in the cloud.*

She would try the bedrooms first. If she found what she needed, the plans said the emergency exit was in the pantry beyond the kitchen. If she didn't—

Her phone beeped with a new text: *Locking!*

A thump from the foyer.

She was out the bathroom door, holding the pistol close to her chest, three fingers around the grip and her index finger on the frame. The Inside Man stood in the middle of the foyer. His shoulders slumped when he saw her gun. "Make it look good," he said, with an almost comical sigh of resignation. "Otherwise—"

"Where's the server?"

His face twisted in confusion. "Look, I don't know where everything is. Hell, they don't even let us go into—"

Twisting her hips, she straight-armed the pistol's barrel into the left side of his jaw, knocking him against the wall. He flopped onto his knees, and she hit him in the same place with the barrel, hard enough to stun and leave a hell of a bruise but not knock him out or fracture his skull. He could tell anyone who cared he'd been pistol-whipped cold.

Once he was down, she zipped his wrists behind his back with one of the riot cuffs from her pocket. Thunder boomed again—no, it was one of the bodyguards pounding on the penthouse's front door, his yells muffled. How long until they figured out how to unlock it?

If she was lucky, she had ten minutes. No, that was far too optimistic. Five minutes at most. She ejected the pistol's magazine and reinserted it, worked the slide. Despite two hard hits to a skull, the mechanism was intact. She moved down the hallway with the weapon in a two-handed combat grip, scanning for the other bodyguard.

The great room offered wraparound views of the Hudson.

Her feet sank to the ankles in thick red carpeting. Enormous couches bracketed a low coffee table roughly the size of her first apartment after college. You couldn't afford a place like this without screwing over the economies of a few smallish countries.

To her right, though the doorway leading to the living room and kitchen, echoed the metallic clink of plates and glasses. She slipped that way. The kitchen was surprisingly narrow, carved from pale marble and blonde wood paneling, with a central island running its length. The bodyguard stood at the island, his back to her as he dumped noodles and chicken from the takeout containers onto plates.

Slipping the pistol into her waistband, she closed the distance to him in three strides. Her shoes too loud on marble. He began to turn, but she snaked an arm around his neck, his throat tight in the angle of her elbow as she pressed the back of his head with her other forearm. He bucked and struggled but she had little trouble rodeo-riding him down. By the time his cheek touched the floor, he was out cold. She riot-cuffed his wrists.

Pulling down her mask, she shoveled a few delicious noodles into her mouth before creeping farther into the kitchen. The pantry waited beyond, its shelves heavy with upscale sauces, olive oil, coffee, candy, and all manner of shiny appliances for chopping, pulverizing, pasta-making. At its far end, the emergency exit: a heavy metal door with a push-bar. No doubt rigged with an alarm.

She returned to the great room, pushing her mask over her face again. The shimmering windows offered a billion-dollar view of the churning darkness over New Jersey, lit from within by strobic blasts of lightning. She crossed to the other hallway and the bedrooms beyond. Paused, trying to listen above the storm.

No creaks or furtive footfalls or whispering. None she could hear above the rain, anyway. Keep moving, she told herself. Through the doorway into a dim hallway. A right into the first bedroom: plush furniture and blonde wood, an enormous bed, nothing resembling computer equipment or a server.

Keep moving. Twenty feet down the hallway to the next door, which was closed. Shifting her pistol to her left hand, she turned the knob as quietly as she could. Click. It was unlocked.

She pushed the door open.

Harsh white light stabbed her eyeballs.

The floor plans had this listed as a bedroom, but the owner clearly had other ideas. A hospital bed dominated the middle of the space, ringed with racks of beeping consoles. Two IV bags dripped clear liquids into the stick-thin arms of a girl lying in the bed. Maybe twelve or thirteen years old? Her eyes were closed, her head shaven, the skin on her neck purpled with fading bruises.

Fiona ducked inside, shutting the door behind her. Nobody else in the room. A white curtain blocked the window. Who was this? The owner's daughter?

The girl's eyes flickered open. Found Fiona's face. Locked on Fiona's gun, widening.

"It's okay," Fiona whispered. "I'm not here to hurt—"

"Help me," the girl whispered. "Get me out of here."

4

NORTH BROTHER ISLAND.

In a city where real estate could sell for thousands of dollars per square foot, this little bump of rock in the middle of Long Island Sound was an oddity: twenty acres of crumbling buildings, thick underbrush, and wildlife. No people allowed.

In the 19th century, North Brother hosted a hospital for isolating folks who suffered from infectious diseases, including Typhoid Mary. In 1904, the steamship *General Slocum* burned to the waterline just offshore, killing more than a thousand sightseers. Fifty years later, a facility for treating heroin addiction opened on the island's northern curve—a laudable goal, except the addicts were often locked up against their will.

The island had many ghosts.

And also a lot of money buried on it—if you believed the rumors.

Bill's folder contained a few old maps of North Brother, along with handwritten notes. The Dean, the insufferable intellectual who ran the Rockaway Mob, had supposedly taken a break from scamming, dealing, and killing long enough to bury a couple million dollars in the island's rocky soil. When Bill worked for the Rockaway Mob, he heard plenty of stories about that cache of cash, but nobody knew the exact location. The Dean was dead, thanks to a series of hilariously bloody events, and Bill had spent the past several months paying stratospheric bar tabs for the motley crew of killers, dumb muscle, and assorted freaks who had once operated in the Rockaway Mob's orbit, hoping they would give him any scraps of information he could use.

Some of those degenerates had told him straight-up lies, street myths that made them sound connected. But others had offered more interesting tidbits. In his handwritten notes, Bill had assembled those scraps into a collage of sorts. He was sure the money was on the island, in one of four possible locations.

He poured another glass of wine, killing the bottle. The wind raked the roof, rattled the windows above the kitchen sink, whipped the small trees on the terrace beyond the bedroom. It was a dark and stormy night, as the cliché went.

There was no regular boat service to North Brother. You could apply for a permit with the Parks Department, then rent a boat to take you on a short hop across the Sound from the Bronx or Queens, but that would mean leaving records in too many systems.

None of which worried Bill too much. For an absurd percentage of the final take, he had secured a boat and a captain who claimed he knew the timing and routes of the NYPD patrols around the island. His friend Max could provide all the equipment they needed to dig.

He checked his phone. Nothing from Fiona.

A warbling overhead, almost like a bird chirping.

He looked up, startled.

A second warble. He tracked the sound to a small, round speaker embedded in a corner of the living room.

"There is someone at the front door," the speaker purred in a British accent.

What a pleasant doorbell, he thought. But who's gently rapping at my chamber door? Some lost soul, perhaps, seeking shelter from the storm? A friend of the house's owner? I can't let them in. It would make things too complicated.

Remember when you've been in trouble? All the times you needed help?

A few minutes ago, he'd been thinking about children. About quitting this wayward life and setting a good example for the next generation. But if you wanted to survive to produce a next generation, a little paranoia never hurt.

Four beeps, followed by the hollow thud of the front door opening. Over the roar of the storm, someone shouted, "Police! We have a warrant!"

Bill slapped his file closed. Could he flee? The house only had one entrance to the street. The garden on the terrace offered nowhere to hide, and nor did any of the rooms. If they were police, they would search every hidey-hole until they found him.

What if they really aren't police?

Such a possibility was even worse. The nearest weapon was a knife he'd used earlier to cut salmon, its blade only three inches long but sharp. A serrated bread knife lay on the cutting board. Not much use against a gun.

Maybe he could bullshit his way out of this. Pouring a glass of wine, he twisted his face into a look of supreme indignation, ready to shout: *How dare you interrupt? Who the fuck are you?*

Two people appeared at the head of the stairs, their waist-length nylon jackets shiny with rain. The man was large and swarthy as a walrus, with a thick red moustache and thinning hair. His blue eyes arctic-cold.

The lady was as compact as her partner was vast, her squared shoulders hinting at serious muscle. Her steel-rimmed glasses, along with her hair yanked back in a tight bun, gave her the severe air of a librarian who enjoyed telling people to quiet down.

They paused to study him, rainwater dripping from their jackets onto the expensive hardwood.

"Police. We have a search warrant," the man said in a conversational tone, pulling a folded paper from his pocket and waving it in the air.

Who executed a search warrant in the middle of a natural disaster? If they weren't cops, it wouldn't be the first time a con artist flashed a random flier or a Chinese takeout menu and said it was a warrant, betting the victim would be too bewildered by the noise and chaos of a search until it was too late. Bill had never pulled such a stunt, but he knew a few thieves who'd tried it at least once.

"Yeah? Let me see it." Bill set his glass down.

"Identify yourself, please," the lady said, her hand on her sidearm.

Bill snorted. "I'm Ralph Barman. Why the hell are you here?"

"Barman?" The man exchanged a look with his partner before turning back to him. "Where's Stephen Jones?"

It took Bill a moment to remember Stephen Jones was the Harvard prick who owned this place. "Europe, the last I heard," Bill said, pairing it with a theatrical shrug. "Anyplace that's not in the path of a major hurricane, am I right?"

"Is there anyone else here?" the man asked.

"No, I'm alone. But I have friends coming over in a bit."

"In this weather?" the man asked, his eyebrows raised.

"They're taking refuge. They live a little too near the water." He sensed the lady watching his eyes and hands.

The man walked toward him, unfolding the paper, and Bill stepped to his right, doing his best to keep the island between them. Not that it would help if one of these jokers drew their gun. The man dropped the paper onto the middle of the island, stepped back, and, with a wave of his hand, invited Bill to examine it.

Keeping the two in his peripheral vision, Bill used a finger to spin the paper around. It looked like a legitimate search warrant, signed by a judge, but how easily could you fake one of those? The warrant listed the address but no property or people to be searched.

"Let me see your badge," Bill said.

The man grinned like he was indulging a petulant child. Reaching into his jacket pocket, he drew his billfold and let it flop open, revealing the badge and ID card. The latter said he was Detective Katzen, John. "Call the station if you want," Katzen said. "We're here on legitimate business."

"I'm Detective Hardaway," the woman said, snapping open her own billfold before pocketing it again. She stepped to the left, peering through the bedroom doorway.

"We're not going to have a problem, are we?" Katzen jutted his chin at the knives near Bill's hands. "You'll notice we've made no move to put you in handcuffs."

"I did notice that. Hard to miss."

"What's your relationship with Stephen Jones?" Hardaway asked.

"You mean, is it sexual?" Toying with cops was always a risk. If you did it right, you could knock them off-balance, force them to play a little nicer. But if they felt disrespected, they might arrest you or smash your face in.

"We're just trying to find where he is," Katzen said. "Remember, we're showing you every courtesy here."

"He's just a friend," Bill said. "He's letting me stay here a few days."

"Do you have any identification?"

"Sure. I'm reaching slowly into my pocket, okay?"

Katzen nodded. He was relaxed, in control, and why not? This wasn't a dark alley. He was in a millionaire's home, interacting with a man who looked like money.

Bill pulled out his calfskin wallet and set his driver's license on the island. If they ran 'Ralph Barman' through the system, it would come back as legitimate. He also had a passport and a set of credit cards with the same name.

Still in the bedroom doorway, Hardaway snapped on a pair of gloves. "Beginning the search," she said.

"Got it," Katzen said, nodding for Bill to return his license to his wallet.

"What are you looking for?" Bill asked.

"That's not your concern," Katzen said. "Just stay right there."

"Sure." If these cops found whatever they were looking for, they would leave. He could settle back onto the couch, free to worry about Fiona.

In the bedroom, glass shattered. Hardaway cursed.

"You okay, partner?" Katzen called out, snapping on his own pair of gloves as he returned to the living room.

"Yeah," Hardaway called. "Nothing in here." A loud thump, followed by the crunch of feet on glass. "There's a bathroom and an office through this door. I'm going that way."

"Got it." Katzen lifted and shook the tchotchkes on the coffee table. Bill had done that earlier, curious if the house's owner had any weed tucked away, but the baubles were solid wood. Katzen moved to the long bookshelf beneath the television and rifled through the books, dumping each on the floor after he was done. They might have been genuine detectives, but something about this operation struck Bill as odd. Didn't cops usually raid multimillionaire pads with a whole team?

One possibility: the cops were genuine, but the search warrant was fake. Whatever they were up to, maybe it wasn't legal—but was it lucrative?

"Perhaps I can help," Bill said.

Katzen spun on him, his eyes bright with frustration. "I told you to stand there and keep your mouth shut."

"You certainly did," Bill said, warming to his theme. "But I'm starting to think you're not exactly here in an official capacity. How'd you know the code for the door?"

It was another risky move, maybe riskier than taunting them. He touched the stump of his left index finger, a gruesome reminder of a time he'd mouthed off to the wrong cop. *Don't push too hard.*

Katzen opened his mouth, ready to speak, when Hardaway returned to the living room. She seemed flustered, her cheeks red, a few strands of hair pasted to her forehead. "There's a safe in the office," she told her partner. "Nothing other than that."

"You wouldn't happen to know the code, would you?" Katzen asked.

"Only if you let me keep half of whatever's inside," Bill said, waiting a breath before adding, "That was a joke."

They offered him murderous glares in return.

"Wow, tough crowd," Bill said.

Hardaway studied Bill's face. "Wait, I know this guy," she said.

An electric shock up Bill's spine. "I'm sure you don't," he said, trying his best to sound confused. "I just have one of those looks..."

"No, I do. It was that task force last year." Her eyes widened. "You're the guy, the Rockaway guy, Bill something," Her hand on her sidearm, her voice rising. "We were going to nail your pelt to the wall and then the Feds stepped in and told us to back off. You..."

"I swear." Bill raised his hands, palms out. "I have zero idea what you're talking about. My name's Ralph Barman and I'm a financial analyst."

But the game was up, because Katzen was nodding, his eyes alight with the righteous fury of an inquisitor who's finally found a sinner to burn at the stake. "You were part of that whole outfit, weren't you?" he said. "The Dean and everyone, all that scumbag cash. Yeah, yeah, I remember your photo. Your name's Bill."

Bill laughed as if he'd never heard anything so ridiculous.

Katzen drew his pistol and aimed it at Bill's head. "For the last time, what are you doing here?"

Bill stared into the pistol barrel, thankful for all the wine keeping him calm. "Sure," he said. "Sure, I'll tell you whatever you want."

5

FIONA STEPPED INTO the weird hospital room and shut the door behind her. The door lacked a lock, so she grabbed a white chair from beside the bed and jammed it beneath the handle. The rain hammered the curtained window. "Who are you?" she asked the girl.

"I'm Jen," the girl said.

"Why are you here?"

Jen squinted. "Why are *you* here?"

No sense in lying. "I'm robbing the place. You don't mind, do you?"

"Heck no." The girl raised her left arm, revealing the handcuff connecting her wrist to the hospital bed's rail. "Just get me out of here, okay? I can…"

"Can what?" How much longer until those bodyguards crashed into the penthouse? The last thing Fiona wanted was a gunfight around a sick child.

"Handle myself," the girl said, offering a brave smile.

The door handle rattled against the chair's back, followed by a whisper from the hallway: "Jen?"

Jen drew her knees up almost to her chest, her face tight with fear.

Fiona stepped to the left of the door and, moving quietly, slipped the chair from beneath the handle. The door opened, pushed by an oddly bluish hand. She gripped it and yanked, dragging into the room a man dressed in hospital scrubs, a surgical mask over his face, his hands snapped into latex gloves.

The man hit the floor knees-first, yelping in pain. Fiona was already on him, slamming the door closed with her foot before planting her knee in the small of his back, driving him onto his stomach. She pressed the pistol into the base of his skull.

"Talk," she said.

"Who the hell are you?" the man wheezed, his arms flailing.

She twisted her leg, driving her knee harder into his spine. "Talk," she said again. "What is this?"

"What is what?" The man took a deep breath. His arms stopped moving, and she sensed him regaining his composure. "Who are you?"

Gripping the back of his neck, she dragged him to his feet. He was quite short, the top of his head level with her sternum, and his eyes were the green of a dead lake. She dug the pistol's barrel into the bridge of his nose, making him blink.

"Who is she?" Fiona asked, nodding toward Jen.

"That's my patient," the man said, his voice tight with rage. "And how dare you—"

She smacked his forehead with the pistol's grip. Not

hard enough to split the skin. "Doctors don't handcuff their patients to beds," she said. "Talk."

"She's here for a transplant," he said.

"And that means she needs to be handcuffed?"

Jen said, "Yeah, it's my kidneys they're taking."

"Who's taking?" Fiona said, shifting her attention to the bed.

Jen snorted. "You think they'd tell me?"

Fiona calculated the odds. The mission would collapse if she attempted some half-assed rescue of a total stranger, but it was halfway to collapse anyway.

Fiona smacked the doctor again. "Key."

With a sigh, he pulled the handcuff key from his pocket. "The rest of the medical team is minutes away. The client is with them. You won't get away with this."

"Key."

He snorted. "You have no idea what you're fucking with."

"You're right. I don't. And I don't care."

"The client owns this girl. Bought and paid for."

She hit him again, harder. This blow left a bright red gash on his forehead. The doctor howled and handed her the handcuff key. She released his collar, letting him fall to his knees while she stepped to the bed and unlocked the handcuffs from Jen's wrist and the rail. While the girl sat up, Fiona returned to the doctor and cuffed his hands behind his back.

"Can you walk?" Fiona asked Jen.

"I think so?" The girl swung her spindly legs over the edge of the bed. When she placed her feet on the floor and tried to stand, her knees quaked, her thighs twitching, and she would have fallen without Fiona dipping forward to grip her elbow.

The doctor struggled into a sitting position.

"Stay down," Fiona told him, plucking the IV lines from

Jen's arms. The punctures bled like crazy. Fiona opened the nearest drawers and found a small box of bandages.

The doctor rose to one knee.

"I can do it," Jen said, taking the box of bandages.

Leaning Jen against the bed, Fiona returned to the doctor. "You know where the server is?" she asked.

"Like, someone who serves food?" His eyes hot and angry.

"Unhelpful." This time she pistol-whipped him to the floor, unconscious.

Her arms covered with bandages, Jen tried standing upright and almost slipped.

"I'll help you," Fiona said, slipping her free arm beneath the girl's armpits, hoisting her up almost on tiptoes. Oh, this was a stupid idea, taking all this dead weight along for the ride. Maybe one of the stupidest ideas in a lifetime full of them. But what choice did she have?

Out into the hallway again. Fiona tried to keep her raised pistol steady, but it was so hard with Jen dragging on her. Through the next door, more bright lights—another bedroom remade into a hospital space, sheets of clear plastic draped from the ceiling around two operating tables pushed together, rows of beeping machines to the left, two refrigerators filled with drugs to the right. Nobody in here. No server, either.

She shut the door, moved down the hallway. Orange light seeped from beneath the next door. Jen moaning softly from all the jostling, biting her lip to keep it in.

"Stay here a second," Fiona said, leaning her against the wall. No crashing or banging from deeper in the apartment. How long could it take them to smash through a door?

Her phone buzzed in her pocket. Probably Fireball, anxious to tell her about something else going wrong.

Pistol in her right hand, she pushed the door open and ducked inside, sweeping the room as she kept her back pressed to the wall. The room was as hideously ornate as the rest of the penthouse, its wood-paneled walls highlighted with gold. A massive desk dominated the middle of the space, bronze sculptures of dragons crouched at either end. She was starting to think the owner wasn't into minimalist design.

She checked the desk. Nothing in its single drawer except two joints and a gold lighter. No sign of a laptop or a phone, much less a server.

Well, this was truly fucked. Maybe the guy had a hidden chamber filled with computer equipment, but she didn't have time to sledgehammer the walls.

A thud shook the room, followed by the clang of metal on marble.

Those meatheads had breached the penthouse's front door. Time to go.

In the hallway again, Fiona grabbed Jen, almost lifting her off her feet. How could a tiny girl be so heavy? Fiona already breathing too hard, her pistol shaking in her grip. The bodyguards hollering deeper in the penthouse, loud over the rumble of thunder.

Into the great room. She had an angle on the entrance hallway and the shattered front door, the silhouettes of the bodyguards swarming. She fired once, twice, three times, aiming high. The thump and howl of men taking cover. She was already through the doorway to the kitchen, breathing ragged now, dragging the kid behind her, hoping her gunfire bought them another minute.

In the pantry, Fiona rammed her shoulder into the exit door, smashing it open, the alarm slamming her ears, Jen shrieking in harmony with it (what a pair of lungs for such a

small body) as they stumbled down flight after flight of concrete stairs. Security right behind and a hurricane incoming—they were dead, so unbelievably fucking dead it was
almost funny.

6

WHENEVER THE PROVERBIAL cow patty really hit the fan, Bill liked to ask himself: WWFD?

What Would Fiona Do?

She was always the harder-headed of the two of them, less given to magical flights of fancy, more likely to plot out a fallback plan, along with a fallback plan for the fallback plan. Fiona had kept them alive in Oklahoma, Cuba, New York, and assorted dens of villainy in-between.

So: What would Fiona do if a corrupt police detective put a gun to her head?

The answer was simple. She would disarm the prick with one of those crazy martial arts moves she spent so many hours practicing, followed by ramming the gun up his tradesman's entrance and pulling the trigger until the weapon clicked empty.

Katzen pressed the pistol's cold barrel against Bill's forehead. "Talk faster."

"I know kung fu," Bill said.

Katzen's eyebrows collided in confusion.

"Actually, scratch that, I don't," Bill said. "I'm basically squatting here. Look, the guy who owns this place, he has some really nice stuff. There's even a gold bust of warrior-poet Tupac Shakur in the office."

"Excuse me?" Katzen said.

"Not exactly the bust of Pallas, but hey, who didn't dig 'California Love' when they were a kid?"

"Do you ever shut up?" Katzen asked.

Bill shrugged. "I'm proud of the fact that I'm making jokes with a gun to my head. Unfortunately, I've had a lot of practice."

"You were with a woman before," Hardaway said. "Is she here?"

For once, Bill was thankful for Fiona's habit of storing her clothing in any available drawers. When Hardaway went through the bedroom, she would have only seen Bill's duffel bag and crumpled shirts. "No," Bill said. "We broke up a long time ago."

Hardaway studied him.

"I'm just squatting," Bill said. "I'm not even part of all that criminal life anymore. Not in a big way, I mean. Even if I told someone about you coming in here, why would they believe me? They'd know I was a liar."

Another old tactic: play into your opponent's perception of you. And these cops bought it. Katzen lowered his pistol. Hardaway's shoulders relaxed. They would leave in a minute or two, perhaps after giving him a warning to depart the premises as soon as the storm passed. He could go back to his wine and worrying about his wife.

Then Katzen's eyes shifted to the folder on the kitchen island.

"What's that?" he asked. "Yours?"

"Just some papers," Bill said. "Nothing huge."

Katzen walked to the far side of the island and flipped open the folder, revealing Bill's notes. "North Brother?" he said. "Why you interested in that place?"

"I'm a history buff," Bill said. "I'd like to visit at some point."

Katzen skimmed the notes. Bill's terrible chicken-scratch was almost impossible to read, but one thing on the first page was terribly clear, written in large block letters: MILLIONS?

"You know we never recovered any of that Rockaway Mob cash, right?" Katzen said, almost to himself. "All those rumors about it buried somewhere."

Bill swallowed. "Everyone in New York's heard those rumors," he said.

"And you think it's here?" Katzen tapped the map.

"I don't know what's there," Bill said. "Like I told you, I'm retired. Just looking for something to do."

Katzen exchanged looks with Hardaway. They had barged in here to kidnap or rob a millionaire, and instead found this hustler drinking in the kitchen. Now they had something like a lead, a hint of money.

"We got to bring them something," Hardaway said.

Bring who *something?* Bill thought.

The lights dimmed and flared. A clanging from outside, as if the wind was hurling something heavy down the street. How long until the storm smashed into the city with full force? No more than an hour at most.

"You're coming with us," Katzen said. "Don't try to resist. Understood?"

"Yes." If he left here, how would Fiona find him? She had once tracked him halfway across the country without him knowing—a bleak time in their relationship, better forgotten. Even in the middle of a storm, she could follow him across the city, provided he left a clue or two. If he distracted these cops long enough, maybe he could send her a text, jot a few words on a scrap of paper—

"Put your phone and wallet and keys on the counter there," Hardaway snapped, as if reading his thoughts. "You so much as twitch wrong, you die."

"Spoken like a true public servant," Bill said, offering her a toothy smile as he emptied his pockets onto the island.

"We'll dig into this more," Katzen said, meaning the notes in the folder, which he snapped closed.

"I need to go to the bathroom," Bill said. There was a small notepad in there, tucked in the medicine cabinet. He could write Fiona a note, stuff it in a bottle, drop the bottle on the floor so she'd notice once she came home, anything—

"You can hold it," Katzen said, waving toward the living room and the door beyond. "Let's go."

WWFD?

Fiona would create lots of opportunities for a pair of crooked cops to screw up. And when they did, she would murder them both. Bill wasn't the biggest fan of violence, always preferring to give someone the hustler's slip—but he'd killed before.

7

FIONA TUMBLED DOWN the stairway, Jen's gangly elbows smashing into her with every step—no time to pull out her phone and call Fireball. It was hard enough keeping a grip on the pistol. Her booming footsteps on the concrete made it impossible to hear the men above her.

First floor, an emergency exit door to her right. She straight-armed the push bar. Nothing. Locked. Two inches of steel separating them from rainy streets and freedom. The wind whistled around the edges of the doorframe. No, not locked. The pressure from the storm held the door closed. She slammed her shoulder against it. Nothing. Again. Nothing. Again. Nothing.

Beside her, Jen pressed her tiny hands against the push bar. Heavy footsteps above. Men yelling. How long did they have? Thirty seconds?

"Keep on it," she told Jen, meaning the push bar, and

backed up until her spine pressed the cold concrete of the opposite wall. She charged, unleashing a banshee scream because why the fuck not, and slammed her weight into the latch bolt. The door banged open an inch, and she rammed her arm through the gap, then her foot, forcing it open against the screaming wind. Rain pelted her face. The girl slipped past her, whining with fear.

The storm was angrier now. Sheets of rain shattered off the sidewalk and filled the gutters with whitewater. Lightning blinked like a photographer's flash at a fashion shoot. Headlights slicing through the gloom—the Toyota SUV rumbling into view, the screaming blur of Fireball behind the wheel, its front tires carving waves through the river rushing down the street.

Jen shivered in her soaked hospital gown as Fiona dragged her to the SUV and tore open the rear door. Yelling from behind them, followed by the loud snap of a gunshot. The SUV's frame sparked beside Fiona's head, the bullet ricocheting into the sky.

"Who the hell is that?" Fireball yelled, ducking. He took his foot off the gas without slamming the brake, the SUV creeping at walking pace as Fiona shoved the wet girl onto the rear seat.

"Fucking drive," Fiona snapped at him, crawling on top of Jen and twisting around—her elbows digging into the girl's ribs, sorry—so she could aim the pistol out the open door. Two of the bodyguards on the sidewalk beside the emergency exit, pistols raised but not firing. Were they afraid of hitting the kid?

Of course. Jen was merchandise, right? You couldn't risk her taking a bullet in one of those very expensive kidneys.

Fiona adjusted her aim, firing a round over their heads,

and they scattered for cover. Fireball screamed, startled by the shot, and stood on the gas pedal. The SUV bolted down the street, skewing into the oncoming lane.

Fiona tucked her legs into the car and pulled the door closed. "Take a left. Go north," she told Fireball as she stripped off her jacket and draped it across the shivering kid, hoping the cheap nylon would preserve that little body's warmth.

Jen's eyes locked on Fiona, wide and aware, evaluating her.

Touching Jen's cheek, Fiona climbed into the front passenger seat, shoving Fireball's oversized laptop into the footwell to make room. Her breathing had slowed. She was unhurt. Everything wasn't totally screwed. Not yet, at least.

"I hope you have a really, really, really good explanation," Fireball yapped, his eyes shifting to the rearview mirror. "Supposed to grab a server, and you come back with a girl?"

"Her name is Jen," Fiona said, flicking the safety on her weapon before holstering it. "They were going to take her kidneys."

"Her what?"

"The organ that cleans her blood. They had a hospital room up there and everything."

"I know what kidneys are, thank you very fucking much." Fireball punched the wheel. "Damn, this was such a bad idea."

Jen swallowed. "It was a good idea to me," she rasped.

"Do you have parents? Someplace we can take you?" Even as the words left her mouth, Fiona realized there was no way they could boot this girl onto a stoop somewhere, goodbye and good luck. Whatever immense forces had brought Jen to a penthouse in lower Manhattan would surely find her again.

Jen shook her head. "I got nobody."

Well, that was a problem to tackle later, after they survived the trip uptown. The SUV slithered in the lane, water splashing over the hood, as Fireball struggled with the wheel. "Let me drive," Fiona told him.

"I got this." He was hunched over the wheel, his nose a few inches from the rain-blurred windshield.

"You definitely don't have this," she said, placing her left hand on the wheel. "Scoot over me. We're not stopping."

Fireball shrugged and took his foot off the gas. Lifting his ass off the seat, he swung toward the passenger side as she slid beneath him. It was a complicated maneuver, but she plopped into the driver's seat and straightened their course. She fluttered the brake to lower their speed, leery of hydroplaning.

In the passenger seat, Fireball retrieved his laptop from the footwell and stuffed it into his backpack, shaking his head as he did so.

"I'm sorry," Fiona said. "I had to do something."

"Did you even look for it?"

"The server? It wasn't there. Or hidden."

"Boz won't throw me shit for work ever again."

"I'll talk to Boz," Fiona said. "In fact, I'll do it right now. Happy?"

"No."

"Aw, turn that frown upside-down." Taking one hand off the wheel, Fiona pulled her phone from her pocket and unlocked it and flicked through the contacts until she found 'JERK.' Dialed. Two bars' worth of signal. Her earbud clicked as the call engaged.

Boz usually plied his miserable trade from an ancient RV parked beneath the BQE overpass in Brooklyn's Sunset Park, but with the hurricane inbound, he had decided to take his chances in Upper Manhattan. If her estimate was correct, Boz was grinding his way uptown, the RV loaded with men and guns and computer equipment, his ultra-expensive speakers blasting disco tripe.

Boz picked up on the third ring. "Yeah?"

"Hey, it's Fiona."

"I bet you wish you were here."

I bet not, she thought. "Why's that?"

"Because we took the time to hurricane-proof the RV. We got armor against debris. We even have a motherfucking snorkel tube poking right up the top, although that's more for the engine's benefit than ours, hopefully. You got my shit?"

"No."

A long pause. No disco music in the background—a bad sign. Boz loved his disco even more than he loved drugs and knives.

"No?" Boz chuckled, but there was no warmth in it, only a promise of pain. "What do you mean, no?"

"We didn't find the server there. There were a lot of guys. Way more than you told me."

"More guys?"

"Yeah, way more. Private security, but the expensive type, not the rent-a-cop type."

"More guys. Why the hell were there more guys?"

Fiona peeked at Jen in the rearview mirror. "I don't know," she said. "And I didn't stick around to find out."

"Any of these pricks see your face? Talk to you?"

"No."

"No?"

"No." She needed him to believe her. "I kept my mask on the whole time."

"You owe me twenty large," Boz said.

"What? Fuck you."

"Nah, you didn't deliver, and I was depending on that data

for big things. I should charge you more, but I'm feeling like a generous fucking dude this evening, given the state of the world, so the price is twenty. And you can forget that other thing we promised you."

The true threat was left unsaid. Boz was a weird guy—you needed a few screws loose in your head to live in a customized RV when your millions could afford a mansion—and like a lot of weird guys, he was an expert at coming up with innovative ways to, in his words, "send a message." That message might involve stuffing someone in an oil-filled barrel or hanging them upside down and bleeding them out like a pig. It all depended on the level of antipsychotics and other meds in his blood at any given moment.

"Who owned that penthouse?" she asked.

"Trust me when I tell you it's better if you don't know. What do you care? You were wearing a mask, right? Twenty large, tomorrow, or your problems only multiply." The call ended with a click.

Fireball stared at her.

"Don't worry," she said. "He didn't say anything about you."

"Doesn't mean squat." Fireball buried his face in his hands.

Before she could offer a witty comeback, lights flared in her side mirror. A car three blocks behind them, coming up fast. Big, like maybe a pickup or SUV. Trouble, most definitely.

8

STEPPING OUTSIDE WAS like plunging into the deep end of a pool. Bill gasped as a thousand gallons of rain drenched him. He lifted his cuffed hands over his eyes in a half-assed attempt to block nature's fury.

Katzen clamped an iron hand on Bill's left shoulder as they hustled him down the sidewalk to a government-issue black car. Stylish, such a vehicle was not, but at least it would have a heater to dry him out—

Hardaway unlocked the car's trunk and lifted the lid, waving for Bill to climb in.

"Oh, come on," Bill said. "You can't possibly—"

Katzen shoved Bill into the trunk with surprising strength. Bill threw out his hands to break his fall, and the cops bent his legs to shove him further into the cramped space.

The trunk slammed shut. Bill lay there, listening to the rain hammer the lid. The thump of doors opening and closing, followed by Katzen and Hardaway murmuring. Bill cocked his head, trying to hear. It was impossible to distinguish words over the storm.

The engine hummed to life, quaking the synthetic fabric beneath him. Sure, he was cold and damp and trapped, but he felt optimistic for the first time since the cops had barged into the house. When you conned folks for a living, you picked up all kinds of esoteric knowledge, like how to escape from car trunks. Virtually all cars built within the past few decades had a handle or cord or switch in the trunk that popped the lid.

The car reversed, then edged from its parking space. Water rumbled beneath the tires. It felt like they were crawling along at two or three miles an hour. Good, good. The speed would make it easier to jump out.

He skimmed his hands across every inch of the trunk—and felt nothing except smooth metal.

This car wasn't that old. Why couldn't he find the release handle or cord or switch or whatever the hell it was? Had the cops taken it out? Which made no sense, either. Regular cops didn't put prisoners in the trunk.

He settled back, concentrating on his breath. Slow in, slow out. This isn't your first time being kidnapped, he thought. Sure, you're cold and shivering, which is a minor issue right now. Do the back seats fold down? You can try, but you'll have to wait until they exit the vehicle.

He paid attention to the car's turns. Right, left, straight for a few minutes, another right. No talking from the front, no music, no static or squawking of a radio. The car rocked on its springs, the wind rising to a screech. They were moving west, close to the Hudson.

You should find a weapon, he thought. Shifting his body,

he worked his fingers beneath the synthetic liner, feeling the spare tire but no tire iron or wrench to split a skull. No, these cops weren't stupid. They wouldn't throw him in here without clearing it of anything lethal.

The car slowed and turned right, thumping over a curb. A metallic rattling. Rain stopped drumming the trunk. The engine cut off, and Bill twisted his body so his coiled legs pointed at the lid. If something bad was about to happen, he could try to kick. It wouldn't help much against a gun, though.

A key rattled in the trunk lock.

The trunk lid rose. Bright lights burned his eyes. He blinked. Behind Hardaway and Katzen stood three men in black rain-jackets, their heads wet, their gazes burning with confusion and barely suppressed rage. He knew their type.

This kept getting better and better.

What's worse than two crooked cops who have no problem with killing you?

How about five crooked cops?

9

FIONA RESISTED THE urge to stomp on the gas. There was too much water on the street. If they hydroplaned, they would crash into the parked cars. She used the mirrors as best she could to pace the black truck behind her, matching its speed. She tried to ignore how badly she wanted to smack Fireball, who was loudly sucking air between his front teeth.

In the back seat, Jen moaned in fear, gripping her seatbelt. She seemed stronger. But was she strong enough for whatever was about to happen? They might need to abandon the vehicle and run.

As they passed an intersection, their pursuer accelerated, headlights flaring, before swerving left over the yellow line. Would they try to come alongside, shoot her through the side window? Not if they were paranoid about a stray round hitting Jen. No, they would try to force her to stop.

"Hold on," she announced, and stepped on the brake,

hoping the truck would overshoot them. If she pulled that off, she could reverse to the last intersection and bang a left, gain a little distance—

The truck slammed into their rear wheel, spinning the SUV around, momentum pushing Fiona deep into her seat, Jen and Fireball screaming like a choir in Hell. They skidded sideways down the street as the truck accelerated again, its enormous chrome grille slamming into her door, its hood inches from her eyes through the cracked glass. Her hands moving on instinct, spinning the wheel so the SUV edged left a fraction. A dirty wave splashing the rear window. She took one hand off the wheel to find her pistol but it was gone, maybe in the footwell or between the seats, and there was no time to search for it before the SUV bumped over a curb and slammed into something hard enough to bang her into the steering wheel.

They stopped.

Steam hissed from gashes in the SUV's hood.

Thank whatever God watched over hooligans and assassins the airbag hadn't deployed, because it might have broken her nose.

The truck's engine roared, the driver trying to reverse, but the bumper must have tangled with the SUV's wreckage. Shaking her head, Fiona tried to see through the tinted windshield. No clue how many men inside.

"There's a subway," Fireball said, brushing bits of glass out of his lap. His shattered window framed the glowing green orb of a subway entrance twenty feet away. The steps descending through the sidewalk to the underworld.

She bent for the gun. Found it by her left foot. "We're moving," she told them. "Your side."

"What? I—" Fireball said, but she had already crawled

over him and slammed open the door with the heel of her hand. Grabbing him by the collar, she dragged him along as she slid over the seats and into the street, her head and shoulders instantly soaked by rain. Fireball squawked in rage and surprise, and because he clutched his waterproof bag with its precious laptop to his chest, he had nothing to break his fall as he landed on the pavement shoulder-first. Fiona was already crab-walking past him to tear open the rear door and pull Jen out. The girl whimpered, her breath hot against Fiona's ear.

"Take her," Fiona hissed, shoving Jen at Fireball.

Fireball had his left arm through one of the backpack's loops, his right arm flailing. "Give me a fucking second, okay?"

"Take her," Fiona growled, pushing the girl into Fireball's arms, forcing him to take the weight. With her hands free, she could work the pistol—no time for a shell check, she'd fired maybe three in the penthouse and another two or three outside, meaning she had three or four rounds left. Did she feel lucky?

I feel like I'm dead, that's how I feel.

She shifted so her weight rested on her left knee. Over the edge of the trunk, she caught a flicker of movement, solid black against the gray sky. The pursuers in the truck were cautious because they knew she had a gun, but they wouldn't hold back for long.

"The subway entrance behind us?" she asked Fireball.

"Yeah?"

"I want you to take her and go there. Fast as you can. Stay low."

"Won't it be closed?"

She didn't have time for this crap. "Do it now."

Fireball splashed away, the girl murmuring something lost in the roar of rain on concrete.

Fiona rose high enough to see through the SUV's rear windows. Through the water-beaded glass, the blurred hulk of the truck, a messy shadow crouched to her left. She raised her pistol and fired once, glass shattering, the shape ducking out of sight.

An answering boom, a wet snap above her head, a blur to her right—the truck's other occupant visible over the SUV's hood, one of the bodyguards from the penthouse, his suit soaked, his right arm raised and flashing white. Boom. Another hole punched in the windshield. She fired, the rainwater in her eyes screwing with her aim. The man yelled and disappeared.

She risked a glance back. Fireball and Jen were almost to the stairs leading down into the subway. She had no angle on the bottom of the stairs, but given how the authorities had closed the system, a gate would prevent them from entering the station. The stairwell would provide some cover, at least.

She scuttled to the left, using the hatchback's rear tire as cover in case someone tried to ricochet a bullet off the pavement and into her ankle. Ammo-wise, she was likely down to one in the chamber.

If she was lucky.

Make it count.

She swooped past the SUV's rear, almost slipping in her sodden shoes. The dead bodyguard lay on his back, raindrops pinging his open eyes. The one with the scar who'd given her so much grief back at the penthouse. Nobody else visible. She rose a few inches, cursing the truck's tinted windows. No movement from inside. She stepped back, keeping her pistol trained on the windows as she swung wide.

If this was an ambush, whoever was inside the truck would have fired by now. Where was the other shooter?

The truck's rear window shattered. The front-passenger window spitting glass as the round passed through. Shooter to the right. She ducked again, risked a peek around the truck's rear bumper. The guy was across the street, crouched behind a mailbox, only the edge of his rain-slick head visible.

The man fired again, the bullet singing into the storm. It was hard to hit your target with the wind roaring down the avenue. If he had the ammunition, he could crouch behind cover and fire at her all day. Make things complicated.

Reaching behind her, she tried the truck's rear door. It opened, and she backed up until her spine pressed against it. Ducked her head into the interior. Nobody inside, as she expected. Just a few greasy bags of fast food on the console, two duffel bags in the rear seat, and what looked like the tip of a police baton poking from the footwell on the passenger side.

The keys still dangled from the ignition.

In another life, she might have climbed in, shut the door, and driven away, leaving Fireball and the girl to their fates. Not today, though. Today she was going to risk death for two people she hardly knew. Didn't that feel good?

"No," she said to herself, slithering into the truck and crawling into the driver's seat. Bending so her head stayed beneath the level of the window, she twisted the key. The truck's engine rumbled.

Now came the fun part, if "fun" meant "a higher-than-average chance of getting shot." She slipped the pistol into her waistband, hoping the guy behind the mailbox wouldn't take this opportunity to charge the truck, and reached across the seats. Plucking the baton from the footwell, she placed it atop the gas pedal, depressing it a fraction. The truck revved.

She moved the shifter into reverse. The truck bucked and crept backwards. She adjusted the wheel slightly, eyeballing the rearview mirror as she did so. No movement from behind the mailbox. Did the guy assume she was trying to get away?

As the truck gained speed, she climbed across the front seats, opened the passenger door, and slid onto the pavement, pirouetting in a crouch so the open door missed her head. Drew the pistol from her waistband. A hollow crunch as the truck plowed into the mailbox, and the guy darted left to avoid two tons of slow-moving metal, his gun raised. She adjusted her aim to account for the wind, pulled the trigger, bang, last round, slide out. The guy tumbled and splashed onto his face.

She stood and filled her hungry lungs with air. One breath, two, three. Nobody on the stormy street. Lots of lit windows overlooking the crime scene, which meant someone was dialing the cops. Both cars were disabled. Running through the storm was a stupid idea—Jen would blow away on a gust of wind before they made it three blocks.

As she stared at the looming buildings, the thousands of lights blinked out for an instant. How much longer would the power last?

She trotted to the body of the guy she'd just shot. Rifled through his pockets, finding an extra magazine of ammo she could use. The guy's wallet contained ninety dollars, which she also pocketed, and nothing else of use.

Returning to the truck, she popped its rear hatch. The pickings included a tool kit, a crowbar and a tire iron, a spare tire, and a length of nylon rope. She helped herself to the crowbar before returning to the other dead man.

She had much better luck with the second corpse. The ammo in his pistol was the wrong caliber and the knife in his hip pocket had a two-inch blade, only good for paring fruit, but in a nylon pouch clipped to his belt she found a DM51 fragmentation grenade.

"Now it's a party," she told the dead man.

Good thing this prick hadn't thrown the little bomb before she shot him.

She returned to the subway entrance. Fireball and Jen hunched before the accordion gate at the bottom, protected from the rain by a concrete lip, their ankles submerged in filthy water. Beyond the gate, the station's lights burned. Maybe an inch or two of water in the hallway leading to the train platform.

"What's going on?" Fireball asked.

"They're all dead," Fiona said, studying the large padlock on the gate. "Go back up for a minute."

"So cold," Jen whispered, her lips blue. Her fingers dug into Fireball's shirt.

"I know, I know," Fiona said, holding up the grenade. "It's only for a minute."

Fireball's eyes widened. "What the hell?"

"Go." She slotted the grenade into the bars above the lock. Slipped a finger through the pin. Waited until Fireball and Jen had ascended back to the street, both kids cursing under their breath. Yanked the pin. Turned and sprinted up the stairs, paranoid of slipping, counting to three in her head.

It actually took four seconds for the grenade to detonate, by which time she was flat on the pavement at the top of the subway stairs, her hands over her ears. The bang of high explosive, followed by a loud rattling she hoped was the gate popping loose of its frame. Crouched beside the hatchback, Fireball and Jen screamed.

Fiona stood, hefting the crowbar, and walked down the stairs to check her work. The padlock pulverized, the gate around it reduced to crazed metal. "Come on," she called.

"Where are we going?" Fireball asked as he escorted Jen down the steps, careful on the wet concrete. His heavy backpack bounced against his spine, the straps too loose.

"No idea," Fiona said. The station would protect them from the rain and wind, at least. With no trains running, they could safely walk the tracks to another station. Hell, it wasn't impossible they could make their way back to the house while staying underground.

But what if the system floods?

You have a point, she told the treacherous demon in her head. Past hurricanes had ruptured tunnels and retaining walls, filling half the subway system with toxic water. For years, politicians insisted they were spending the money to ensure such a thing never happened again, but since when could you trust anything they said?

She would just have to risk it. And yet she hesitated at the top of the stairway, frozen by a vision of whitewater foaming down a tunnel, sweeping away anything in its path, drowning anyone foolish enough to try and take refuge deep in the earth...

A rising growl from the street. She ran up the steps. Two black SUVs barreled around the corner of Houston. The reinforcements had arrived. Gripping the wet crowbar, she scrambled back to the broken gate, hoping she had enough time to force it open.

10

ONE OF THE cops reached into the trunk and pulled Bill out in one smooth motion. Bill barely had time to throw his arms in front of his face before tumbling to the oil-stained concrete.

"This ain't the Wall Street dude," another cop barked.

Bill rose to one knee, waiting to see what happened next. The cops stared at him. Bill stood and straightened his wet lapels. "Good evening," he said, hoping it sounded cool and nonchalant instead of terrified to death.

"This might be better," Katzen said.

"Might? I don't like 'might,'" replied the cop who'd pulled Bill from the trunk. He was almost seven feet tall, with the thick neck and shoulders of someone who deadlifted pickups for fun. The swirling black tendrils of a tattoo poked from the edge of his collar.

"His name's Bill," Hardaway said, her footsteps echoing on

concrete as she walked across the warehouse. Bill, tracking her path, noted the line of cars parked against the far wall: two black sedans, a police cruiser, and the enormous hulk of an armored personnel carrier with 'SWAT' stenciled on its side. A few official-looking placards bolted to the walls. If Bill had to guess, they were in a police depot.

"What's Bill have to do with anything?" growled one of the other cops, an equally massive dude with a shaved head and a tuft of gray hair on his bulldozer-square chin.

"He was part of the Rockaway Mob," Katzen said, raising Bill's folder. "We found him with a map of North Brother Island. There might be money there."

"There's that 'might' again," the tattooed cop said, shaking his head. "I don't fucking like this, you understand?"

"I'm retired," Bill said. "Out of the game entirely."

"Shut up," Hardaway snapped.

Bill scanned the metal rafters and spotted five CCTV cameras, no doubt disabled. A steel door in the wall to his right, maybe leading to an office; straight ahead, three roll-up doors, large enough to admit the armored personnel carrier, led to the outside. In the middle of the space, in the harsh glow of the caged lights, stood a long table littered with fast-food bags, tools, handheld radios, and coils of rope and electrical cords. He counted three power drills and a collection of screwdrivers, along with a taser and a small blowtorch.

Whatever they'd planned for the Wall Street dude, it wasn't a sing-along.

Closer to the far wall, another folding table featured a sleek silver coffee machine, a stack of porcelain mugs and paper cups, and a plastic box filled with disposable coffee pods. Its presence made sense. Who hasn't wanted a few jolts of caffeine when torturing hostages late into the night? These guys had thought of everything.

Hardaway grabbed one of the folding chairs propped against the torture table and returned to the group. She popped the chair open, then reached beneath her jacket and extracted her handcuffs.

"What you have to say for yourself, Bill?" asked the third cop, an older guy with a snow-white crewcut and the black eyes of a shark. "You know about some money?"

"Give me some dry clothes and we'll talk," Bill said, shaking his arms for emphasis, hoping to scatter some water onto these cops who were standing too close. They all took a step back to dodge his spray. Good enough.

Thunder roared loud enough to make the metal roof hum. Katzen offered it a wary glance before jabbing the side of his foot into Bill's shin. "Tell them."

Bill almost stumbled. Placing a steadying hand against the car trunk, he straightened again, noting how the tattooed cop gave Katzen an irritated look.

"It's true, I used to work for Rockaway," Bill said. "I did some money stuff for them. The Feds kicked me loose when…"

The cop with the soul patch snapped his fingers. "Oh yeah, when that building burned? That pot farm up on that roof?" He chuckled. "Half of Queens got a contact high off that shit."

"Get to the money," Katzen said. "We don't have all night."

"The Dean—that's the guy who ran the Rockaway Mob, as I'm sure all of you fine gents know—buried twenty million in a bunch of bags. It's on North Brother Island." Bill pointed at the ceiling and the storm beyond. "Which means we'll have to wait 'til after all this passes to get it."

"Shoulda stuck to the plan," the tattooed cop muttered. "Shoulda just grabbed Stephen…"

"He wasn't there, so the plan was fucked," Katzen snapped. "This is the new plan."

Bill decided to name these cops after their distinguishing features—Tattoo, Soul Patch, and Crew Cut. Tattoo struck him as the angriest, quick to snap off. Soul Patch seemed like he had more of a brain, which made him unpredictable. Crew Cut was a senior member, maybe with an inflated ego to match, but it was too soon to tell.

"Where on North Brother?" Soul Patch asked Bill.

"He's got a couple sites picked out in this folder," Katzen said.

"And those are only guesses. What's in that folder, it's maybe half the intelligence I picked up." Bill tapped his forehead. "The rest is in here. You'll just have to take me there."

"You'll talk if we yank your fucking teeth out," Tattoo said.

"Our new friend Bill's been tortured before," Hardaway said. "See that stump where he had a finger? Bill, you want to come over here, have a seat?"

"Do I have a choice?" Bill asked.

"You definitely do not." Hardaway patted the chair. "Come on."

"We can get it out of him," Tattoo said.

"Sure, torture my ass." Bill plopped on the folding chair. He would never admit it to these grunts, but it felt good to sit. Too much fear and adrenaline had turned his knees to gelatin. "You know how it'll go? I'll say whatever just to make it stop. And then you'll kill me, but you won't know whether I was actually lying or not. It's better to take me out there. If you're going anyway."

"He's not wrong," Katzen said.

"Even if we take this at face value, and even if we decide to do it—and both of those are some pretty big fucking 'ifs'—we can't get out there tonight," Soul Patch said, bouncing on the balls of his feet.

Bill tilted his head, listening to the steady rain on the roof, the thrum of the enormous lights overhead. This place was built solidly enough for everyone to talk at a conversational level despite the storm of the century roaring overhead. And hurricane or no, he guessed there was enough concrete and steel to stop anyone outside from hearing screams or gunshots.

Thunder boomed.

"Hear that? You're fucking nuts," Hardaway said. "We just drove through it, and it's getting worse. We'll wait a few hours until this storm passes…"

"That's when everyone will come outside. There'll be too many fucking witnesses," Soul Patch said. "Nobody's out there right now. I got friends in Harbor Patrol. We might have to cut them in, but it wouldn't be much."

Crew Cut raised a hand. "We'll wait until the storm passes. It's safer. A couple more hours won't matter, unless Bill has anyone looking for him. Anyone looking for you, Bill?"

Bill shook his head.

"Call your guy," Crew Cut told Soul Patch, before turning to Bill. "And I swear, if you're lying to us, we're going to leave you on that island in pieces, am I clear?"

"Absolutely," Bill said, relieved despite Crew Cut's promise of butchery. He'd guessed right about the older man being a leader, as well as Tattoo's hair-trigger temper. Soul Patch was impulsive. And if any of these five cops hated each other, it could yield pure opportunity. He could work the seam, split it open.

Hardaway yanked Bill's arms behind his back. The cold pinch of metal as the handcuffs snapped over his wrists. "Just try us," she muttered in his ear.

11

THE RUINED GATE tore from its rusty hinges. Fiona pushed it aside before tossing the crowbar to Fireball and wrapping an arm beneath Jen's armpits, the girl shivering against her. They scurried down the hallway leading to the platform, Fiona trying to listen above the storm for footfalls on concrete, yelling, anything to indicate pursuit from above.

The stationmaster's kiosk was empty. Fiona peeked through the scratched windows. Nothing of interest on the desk, just papers and a crushed jumbo can of energy drink. She tried the door. Locked. Besides, even if it wasn't, would a stationmaster have anything useful? It wasn't as if the MTA equipped its station employees with a machine gun, which was the one thing she needed at this juncture.

"Take her," she said as she passed Jen to Fireball. Jen coughed, a brutally loud sound that echoed off the station tiles.

"I hope to all that's holy you got a plan," Fireball said, struggling to hoist Jen. "Because if you don't—"

"Wait here." Fiona leapt the turnstiles.

"Wait," Fireball said, his panic rising. "You're not leaving us here, you hear me? You're not—"

Fiona walked over to the emergency exit door and opened it. "As tempting as that might be," she said, waving for Fireball to drag Jen through. From this angle, she had a view down the station hallway almost to the base of the stairs. Why hadn't anyone come down? Maybe they thought she had another explosive or two.

Well, let them think so. She did a mental shell count: full clip, plus the crowbar. Not great, but not terrible, either. Despite her soaked clothes, she didn't feel cold. Thanks, adrenaline!

"We could cross the tracks," Fireball said, pointing to the opposite platform. "Go out the other exit."

"Probably got a gate," Fiona said.

Jen coughed again, loud, explosive. A string of snot swung from her nose. "This day sucks," she wheezed, wiping her nose with the back of her hand.

"I've had worse," Fiona said.

"I haven't." Fireball pointed to the tracks. "We go down there, I guess? Better hope they're not lying about the trains not running." His teeth chattering softly. The poor guy had played thousands of hours of first-person shooters throughout his wayward life, gunning down millions of baddies with an impressive array of oversized guns. Well, reality never offered the kindnesses of a respawn point and the ability to save your game.

"Yeah," Fiona said, not enthused about the idea, but what

choice did they have? "We'll head uptown. Get back to the house, we can regroup, think this through."

"And a drink," Jen said. "I could use a drink."

"What are you, twelve?" Fireball asked.

Jen sneered at him. "I'm joking, dumbass."

"At least you're feeling good enough to screw with him," Fiona said. The girl wasn't strong enough to move on her own, but she wouldn't drop dead on them. And right now, such things counted as a big win.

Fiona waved for them to follow her to the north side of the platform, where a waist-high gate blocked off the maintenance walkway running along the side of the tunnel. She paused there, one hand on the gate, listening and smelling. No distant squeal of subway wheels on tracks, no rumble of floodwaters. The tracks clear aside from a stream of pungent sludge on the bottom. Not even any rats—did they know something she didn't?

She pulled out her phone and flicked on the flashlight app, praying she had enough battery life to last however long they needed to spend in this tunnel. She pushed through the gate, flicking the light over the narrow walkway, Fireball and Jen close behind her.

The walkway ran for another thirty feet before ending in a short ladder to the tracks. To their right, a small alcove and a metal door without markings on it. She tried the handle. Locked. Likely led to a maintenance shaft.

A prickling unease—a signal from deep in her lizard brain, warning her to watch out.

"Hold on," she whispered, clicking off her phone's light.

"What's wrong?" Jen asked, her voice echoing off the tunnel's concrete curve.

"Hush," Fiona said, pressing her body against the walkway

railing so she could see beyond them, back into the station. The tunnel's entrance framed the platform and the edge of the turnstiles. Nothing seemed different from a minute or two ago, except for a trickle of water from the ceiling above the turnstiles, pattering off the concrete. Had that perked her attention?

No, the dripping had nothing to do with it.

She was holding her breath. She exhaled slowly, sucked down more oxygen and held it. Leaned further over the railing, hoping for a better angle of the station—

Yes, there. Poking from just above the turnstiles, a tiny black... dot. Like the tip of a gun barrel, pointing across the tracks toward the opposite platform. Like someone was standing on the far side of the turnstiles, scanning for danger before making a move.

No, you're paranoid.

I'm not, she told the demon in her head. I'm most definitely not.

She raised the pistol. If their pursuer showed a little more of themselves, she could risk a shot, but she had no idea how many hunters were down here. The tunnel offered no cover, nowhere to hide if they came in this direction.

The black dot edged forward, becoming the stubby barrel of a submachine gun held by thin, pale hands. The arms holding the gun appeared beyond the edge of the turnstiles, clad in shiny raingear. Then the body, the head hooded, the legs encased in soaking-wet jeans. Smaller than Fiona expected. A woman, maybe?

The hooded figure climbed over the turnstiles and onto the platform, sweeping the gun along the tracks. "Clear," it said in a high-pitched voice—a woman, yeah—before turning back and opening the emergency exit.

Three more figures stepped onto the platform, clad like the first in soaking-wet raingear and jeans, all armed with submachine guns with extended clips. Fiona bet those weapons were converted to automatic fire. The way they spread out across the platform, covering every angle, suggested they were professionals—certainly more skilled than the chumps in the penthouse or the two bodyguards she'd gunned down beside the truck.

Great.

She tapped Fireball's shoulder and, when he looked at her, placed a finger to her lips. Gestured for him to climb down the ladder to the tracks—but quietly.

Fireball nodded. Moving as slowly as he could, he lifted Jen off his shoulder and passed her to Fiona, who pivoted, placing the girl against the concrete wall. Jen's breath loud in her ear.

Fireball set the crowbar on the concrete and placed his hands on the railing and his left foot on the first rung. His backpack straps creaked.

His foot scraped the rough metal, frighteningly loud.

Fiona tensed. Two of the armed men stood at the downtown side of the platform, sweeping their guns along the tracks. The others clustered at the turnstiles, their heads tilted together. The murmur of conversation.

Fireball descended another rung.

One of the men sat on the edge of the platform, his legs dangling over the tracks.

Fiona waved for Fireball to move faster. Jen's hand on her shoulder, Jen moving past her, placing a shaky hand on the railing, looking at Fiona like: Should I do this?

Fiona nodded.

Jen placed her first foot on the rung. Her leg shaking.

Fireball, already at the bottom, placed a light hand on her hip, trying to steady her.

Jen stepped to the second rung. The ladder tapped against the concrete—*ping!*

The sitting man pushed off, landing on the tracks, and the man above him passed down a rifle. The others near the turnstiles wandered to the platform's edge, slinging their weapons across their backs.

What would happen now? If Fiona was lucky, they would sweep the downtown tunnel as a squad, leaving her to retreat uptown with the kids. But she wasn't so lucky. If these hunters had half a brain between them, they would split into two groups and hit both the uptown and downtown tunnels.

Which left the question: How far would they explore before turning back?

Jen settled on the last rung, Fireball's hands around her waist. Their breath loud, rapid, panicked. Too damn loud.

Fiona kept her gun aimed at the man who stood on the tracks. The others descended from the platform one at a time, the rest providing cover. Did they have flashlights? Probably. They were prepared.

The station lights dimmed and flared.

Imagine being down here if the city lost power. If a retaining wall gave way and the system flooded. Lost in the blackness, cold water pushing against your feet, then your legs, then your waist. Filling your lungs. Sucking you down. Fiona didn't want to think about it. She started to climb down the ladder—a tricky business with the pistol in one hand. She tried lowering her feet as slowly and quietly as possible onto the tracks, but she missed and her left foot slid into the toxic mud with a squish broadcast in stereo, drowned out by the clink and rustle of hunters shifting because they heard, they knew, they were ready to—

She raised the pistol.

The hunters paused.

These guys weren't the bodyguards from the penthouse. They were dressed differently, moved differently. But they shared one big similarity, she realized.

They wouldn't fire wildly into the tunnel. Too much risk of hitting Jen.

That wouldn't stop them from getting close enough to shoot Fiona in the head at point-blank range, though.

Lovely.

One of the hunters took a step toward the tunnel entrance—only for his nearest companion to hiss a question. The lead hunter turned back, joining heads again in urgent discussion.

Fiona waved for Fireball to walk deeper into the tunnel. Mimed stepping carefully from wooden crosstie to crosstie. Beside him, Jen wrinkled her nose at the stench.

Fireball took Jen's hand (it really was sweet, how he was watching over her) and stepped to the first crosstie, testing the wood with the edge of his toe before settling his full weight on it. Jen followed, her bare feet tapping the crosstie, testing for splinters, before she committed.

The wood creaked.

One of the hunters stepped toward the pillars separating uptown from downtown tracks. The hood hid the face except for a pale curve of chin, but the figure moved with a catlike grace, a confidence that suggested they could handle themselves in a fight.

Two of the others followed the first one, rifles raised. The remaining one knelt on the tracks and faced the downtown tunnel, ready for whatever might come in that direction.

None of them had flashlights, Fiona realized. One small advantage.

Jen clapped her hands over her mouth, her eyes widening in panic.

Fiona jabbed a finger at her: *Don't you dare cough.* Jen's throat jerked as she tried to hold it in.

The hunter trio at the tunnel entrance now, maybe twenty yards away, maybe ten seconds from running into them if they kept their pace.

And now Fiona heard a most peculiar sound from deeper in the tunnel, a low whistling that rose and rose, and her guts clenched as she thought *train* but this was something different, not the screech of metal on metal but air fluttering fleshy vocal cords, warping into notes so familiar and yet ever-so-slightly off-key, a radio hit from long before Fiona was born—

To Fiona's left, against the tunnel wall, emerged a figure almost impossible to see, black on black except for the ghostly splotch of the face. The smudge of what might have been arm rising, as the whistle sharpened into a snapped command:

"*Get down.*"

Grabbing Fireball and Jen by the collar, Fiona dove between the crossties. Her knees splashing in mud, the stink of the subway filling her nostrils. In front of her stepped a man in dark combat gear, his hair upswept in a gravity-defying pompadour, in his grip an ancient submachine gun that probably last saw action in France during World War II.

"*Hunka hunka,*" the man said, and pulled the trigger. In the enclosed tunnel, the roar of ammunition was ear-bursting, apocalyptic, and Jen screamed against Fiona's armpit as bullets snapped over their heads.

Fiona knew this guy.

Except it was impossible. The man was dead. By her hand, no less.

Dead or not, the guy paused long enough to eject the gun's newly empty magazine before slapping in a fresh one. At the tunnel entrance, the hunters had taken cover behind the pillars.

"Better get a move on, little ones," the man snapped, jerking his head behind him, and pulled the trigger again. Grabbing Fireball and Jen by the arms, Fiona peeled them from the mud and pushed them deeper into the tunnel lit by gunfire.

REWIND:
BEFORE THE STORM

I WAS LOADING a week's worth of water, energy bars, and fatty snacks into the trunk of my car when Battlin' Bob Blazinsky, a small-time thug with a plus-sized appetite for booze and beating people down, phoned me with a last-minute assignment to break someone's legs. I still wasn't used to taking requests from a tiny fish like Bob, whose criminal "empire" extended for two whole blocks of St. Mark's Place. Every time he sent me to snap a bone or break a nose, I wanted to inform him in my snootiest possible tone that I had once been more—so much more.

But even had I informed Bob about the time I killed three Sicilian elders with a popsicle stick at an outdoor café in Capri, I doubt he'd have the mental capacity to be impressed. Bob couldn't find Italy on a map—or the Empire State Building, for that matter. To preserve whatever was left of my sanity, I kept my mouth shut whenever he handed me a greasy wad of twenties like he was a king conferring the grandest of gifts upon a humble subject.

"Yeah, need those skills of yours," Bob grunted over the phone. In the background, I heard the buggy buzz of tattoo guns, so he was sitting in his makeshift "office" in the rear of the Tat Cat.

I slammed my trunk closed and swiveled for a panoramic look at the street. It was, as you might expect in the hours before a major hurricane made landfall, an incredible shitshow. I imagined the citizens of other states, confronted with the prospect of disaster, packed their cars with supplies, water, tents, and whatever else they might need to survive for a few days. Contrast that with the happy folk of New York City, or at least the Village, intent on stuffing their vehicles with liquor, cigarettes, books, small dogs, baggies of weed and pills, and their finest clothes.

"You take a look outside?" I asked him.

"Uh, yeah?"

"Hurricane's coming, so I'm leaving. Probably take me five hours to get across the bridge."

"Oh, come on." Bob could adopt a whining tone unsuitable for someone who imagined himself as Al Capone's successor. "The guy's close, I swear. I'll throw in a little extra, okay?"

Metal crunched. At the intersection, two sedans pirouetted in a glittering spray of glass and paint. Bystanders paused to raise their phones, hoping to record a good fight.

"How much we talking?" I asked.

"Guy owes me two."

"And you're paying me what?"

"The usual?"

"No." I glanced at the sky thick with scuttling clouds. "Three hundred this time, man. That's crunch rates."

"You're fucking kidding me." Anger now. He thought it made him sound intimidating, but I had to resist the urge to snort. *Maybe I should've told him about the time I took on an entire Oklahoma town with a pair of AK-47s and lived to tell the tale.*

"I kid you not," I said. "You don't like it, find someone who'll do it cheaper. Who you got there in the tattoo parlor? Goth Queen and the Lube King? They'll do it if you teach them how to use a bat."

By the way Bob hissed, I knew he had nobody right now.

As I waited for him to collect his thoughts, I watched the drivers of those crashed cars circle their wreckage, pointing and cursing. More cars tried to squeeze past the wrecks, but it was a tight fit, and traffic began to clog the street in both directions.

"Fine," Bob said. "Three hundred, but you make sure that leg is good and broken, you understand? I want that kid to limp for the rest of his natural life."

"I'll bend it around like a swizzle stick," I said. "What are his details?"

"Guy's name is Alec," Bob said. "Young guy, blonde, looks like a real frat boy. Can't bet on football for shit, either. He's drinking over at The Shrunken Head right now."

"How do you know that?"

"The bartender." Bob sounded almost insulted. "The bartender owes me."

"Fine. You better stick around in the tattoo parlor," I said. "I'll be around shortly for the money."

"Wait. How'd you know I was at—"

I ended the call. It was time to admit that driving up to my little shack was a bad idea. I could walk the two blocks to The Shrunken Head, teach this kid a lesson he'd never forget, pick up my cash, and lock myself in my apartment before the storm hit. Ride out the hurricane in comfort, provided the wind refrained from sending a van through my bedroom window.

Or I could skip the beatdown and lock myself in my humble abode, sparing me the whining and screams of yet another poor sap who thought the Buffalo Bills had a chance of winning against anyone this season other than a high school team. But I needed to pay the rent, and hurting people was one of my few marketable skills, along with bad jokes and mixing a halfway decent drink. I didn't feel terrible about it. It wasn't like I was killing anybody.

The Shrunken Head was packed with drunken lunatics in the middle of the day. Never mind an oncoming hurricane or yet another fast-spreading pandemic—they stood shoulder-to-shoulder, sweating in the windowless murk, pounding down shot after shot of sugared engine cleaner. The speakers bolted above the liquor shelves blasted a droning, repetitive beat that technically qualified as music. I thought it sounded more like a factory machine on the verge of blowing a gasket.

I elbowed my way to the bar and caught the bartender's eye. He had the wrinkled face and wary gaze of someone who had survived the Village in all of its permutations over the decades, from the tragically hip warzones of the Reagan era to the weird silence of the Covid years.

When he approached, cocking his head, I leaned across the bar and said, "Bob sent me."

The bartender slammed his elbows on the bar and entered my airspace until we were almost nose-to-nose. "Men's room," he hissed. "White t-shirt with a green face on it. Do me a favor? You got to tune the guy up, don't do it in there."

Whatever. I nodded, slapped a twenty on the bar, and

surfed upstream through the crowd. In the back, a short hallway led to the restrooms. It was empty but wouldn't stay that way for long.

I knocked on the door of the men's room. From many sad hours spent in The Shrunken Head, I knew it was a single-stall deal.

"Out in a sec," someone yelled back.

"Hurry up," I said.

The door lock thumped. I took a half-step back, my right hand balled into a fist. When the door opened a crack, I glimpsed a kid fitting the bartender's description. I rammed the door with my elbow, slamming it open, and the kid stumbled back, his arms windmilling as he tried to regain his balance.

I slipped through the door, slammed it closed, threw the lock.

"What the fuck?" the kid yelled, recovering his balance. He hopped onto his toes like a boxer warming up, his hands balled in front of his chest. "What the fuck, man?"

"We have to talk," I said.

The kid swung at me. It was a loose punch I saw coming from a mile away, and it was easy enough to deflect it with my forearm before rabbit-punching him in the nose, my usual opening gambit. I was always interested in what happened afterwards. Tougher people will spit the blood and launch at you again, but most folks will surrender.

The kid clapped his hands over his nose and howled. Now I was thankful for the annoying music shaking the walls, which lessened the chances of anyone overhearing his screams. The howl quieted to a gurgle, followed by a sniff. The kid lowered his hands from his bloody nose and wheezed, "What the fuck?"

"Bob sent me," I said. "You owe him two large."

"I don't have it."

I rolled my eyes. "Don't be boring."

He squinted. "What?"

"They all say that. 'I don't have it.' But you knew this was coming, right? That someone like me would show up?"

"I guess." He shrugged. "I mean, getting beaten up, that's just in those old mob movies, right?"

I looked at him again—really looked at him, from the spray of acne across his forehead to the red edge of the new tattoo poking from the left sleeve of his ridiculous t-shirt. He was barely old enough to drink. "Kid," I said. "Is this your first time borrowing money from a guy like Bob?"

He nodded.

"Okay." God, this was so distasteful. "Okay, listen up. It's not like borrowing from a bank or one of those stupid money apps. It's not like you rack up interest payments or something like that. Wait," I squinted at him, "didn't Bob explain any of this to you?"

The kid shook his head. Whatever allowed him to maintain his composure was starting to break down. His lower lip quivered, and his hands fell to his sides. He looked more than ever like a scared little child.

Someone knocked on the door behind me. The knob rattled.

"Still in here," I called.

"I used one of those apps," the kid said, haltingly, but then the words came in a rush: "I needed the money and the app would only give me five hundred bucks so I asked my friend Jeremy, I said, 'Hey, where can I get some cash,' and he said, 'Dude, there's this scary guy over on St. Mark's, I used him when I had to get some cash for weed but you got to pay him back, dude,' and I was like, 'Dude, okay, I'll pay him back, don't worry,' and so I went and borrowed two grand for the ring and..."

"Wait." I raised a hand. "You didn't bet on the game?"

"Game?"

"The money," I sighed. "You needed it for a ring?"

The kid dug into his hip pocket, his hand emerging with a gold ring topped with a tiny diamond. "Melanie wants to get married," he said. "I had to do it. She's so friggin' hot. You can see for yourself, she's at the bar..."

I'd done it all wrong. In all these months since I returned from Oklahoma, I told myself breaking folks' bones was a good thing if it meant no more killing. Except that wasn't true, was it? Whatever your feelings about the act of murder, all of those clients had it coming, one way or another. And death itself is nothing to be afraid of—trust me.

But this? Tracking down deadbeats who were dumb or desperate enough to borrow a little bit of cash at an absurd interest rate from a dude who looked and acted like a reject from a bottom-rate reality show? How undignified—for them, and for me. We could all do better.

I raised a hand. "Okay, reset."

The kid's eyes brimmed with tears and idiotic hope.

"I'm going to spare you, but you have to promise me something."

He nodded harder. "Anything."

"You go out there and propose to her right now."

He winced. I could understand why. The Shrunken Head was no place to propose to a lady of any caliber. "That's it? That'll clear the debt?" he asked.

I shrugged. "Why not?"

He laughed and wiped his mouth again. "Oh dude, I don't know how to thank..."

"Don't thank me," I said. "Please. I can't take it." I unlocked the door. "Let's do this before they kick the door in."

I opened the door, and the dude on the other side of it—a hipster with a wisp of a goatee and a pageboy cap—backed up and snapped, "Get a *room*."

I smiled at him. The kid scuttled past me, the ring clutched in his fist, practically crowd-surfing through the scrum of drunkards toward a petite redhead sitting by the windows. My attention flicked to the television above the bar, which displayed a map of the Eastern Seaboard and the giant crimson blotch churning offshore of Maryland. It was Armageddon, not that anyone in here cared.

The redhead screamed with her hands clapped over her mouth. The boy knelt before her, ring held high, its diamond gleaming in the multicolored Christmas lights strung along the ceiling, and her joy triggered a chain reaction throughout the bar, a hundred drunks and lunatics roaring in harmony that would have done a choir director proud. The boy's face suffused with the pure bliss you experience maybe once or twice in your life. As the redhead screamed again and fell to her knees on the beer-sticky floor and embraced him, I felt an explosive longing for something like that to happen to me, a transcendence blasting away all the grime and nastiness of my life, and—

I shoved my way through the crowd and out the front door. As I passed the bartender, he mouthed: *What the fuck?* I responded with a slight shrug. Just another crazy day in the Big City, huh?

On the street again, I found my thoughts returning to Oklahoma. My new friends Bill and Fiona in a barn full of old guns, helping me choose exactly the right weapons to vaporize the crowd of evil rednecks swarming our position. *Us three, we're a brutal bunch of heartbroken saps*, I told them. *And we need all the help we can get.* Bill and Fiona had found a happy ending, but what did I get? What do you do after you've vaporized every particle of your old life?

It took five minutes to walk to Bob Blazinsky's rundown headquarters. If you wanted a cheap tattoo needled by an artist with questionable drawing skills, you couldn't do much better than the Tat Cat, which competed on price rather than quality. I entered to find its three tattooing stations empty, Goth Queen and the Lube King perched at the rear counter with an open bottle of whiskey between them.

Goth Queen was a short woman in a Victorian funeral dress, her black haircut like a helmet framing her small, round face. She was an okay artist, provided you wanted something that looked like it was drawn during an earthquake, and a better hustler. The Lube King, meanwhile, was huge and bald and preferred shirts that exposed as much of his skin as possible, the better to show off his elaborate tattoos. I had no idea why they called him the Lube King, and absolutely no urge to find out.

"Where is he?" I asked.

"I'm right here, buddy." Bob stepped from the doorway leading to the back office, wiping his broad hands on his cargo pants. His gut strained against a canary-yellow polo shirt, his hair swept back so tightly against his skull it pulled the skin of his face taut.

"It's a good thing mirrors can't laugh," I said.

"What?" Bob snapped. He marched forward, offering his best attempt at a hard glare.

"I didn't do it. You got to forgive the kid's debt, too," I said.

"I don't know what might have gone on, but he didn't know what he was getting into."

"The fuck do I care?" he growled, except the last syllable rose in a whine.

"You don't have to care," I said, walking as nonchalantly as I could toward the nearest tattooing station. Bob closed the space between us at a rapid clip, but I had plenty of time to scan the bottles and containers for exactly what I needed.

The Lube King stood, his hands loose at his sides, ready to back Bob's play. I had no idea if he did anything criminal for Bob, and frankly, it didn't matter. Unless he was a serial killer with a serious body count and a mastery of a chainsaw, chances were excellent I could take him in a fight.

"The kid used the money to buy an engagement ring," I continued. "I think that's worth taking into consideration."

"I don't give a *shit*," Bob said, almost close enough to grab me, his face a fetching shade of heart-attack red edging into purple. Spittle flew from his lips and speckled my cheek.

"Okay," I said. And as he approached, his hand rising, I snatched his thumb and twisted it hard, his arm corkscrewing with it, followed by his whole body. He squawked in surprise and fear as I slammed him against the wall, his bones on the verge of fracture.

"Don't," I told him.

"Get him off," Bob wheezed, still trying to ease his way out of my grip, but the fight had already drained from him.

"I've killed around two hundred people," I said, my tone conversational. "I've killed them around the world. I've killed folks who begged for their lives and folks who took it like a champ. I've killed folks with pretty much every single kind of tool and gun you can imagine, including a stuffed teddy bear, which, believe me, is just as messy and annoying as you'd think."

The Lube King looked in my eyes and knew I was telling the truth. He backed up a step. Behind him, the Goth Queen had already grabbed her spike-studded purse from under the counter and slung it around her shoulders.

"I want that duct tape," I told her, jutting my chin toward a roll of it on the counter. I raised my free hand, and she tossed it to me.

"Now leave," I told them. "Lock the door behind you."

"Look," Bob said. "We can talk about this."

"I'm done talking," I said.

The Lube King and Goth Queen left, never looking back. When the lock clicked in the front door, I shoved Bob onto the nearest tattooing chair. He flopped onto the plush surface like a fish ready for gutting. He lifted a hand, maybe to fight, but I was already on him again, duct-taping his wrists to the chair's arms. He tried to kick, and I mummified his lower body with the rest of the roll.

"I'm sorry," he babbled. "I'm sorry, okay? You should have let me know."

"Nah," I said evenly. "I'm the one who's sorry. I was trying to turn a new leaf, but I didn't think inventively enough in terms of career choices."

He squinted in confusion. "Huh?"

I picked up the nearest tattoo gun. I had spent enough time in the Tat Cat to have a general idea of how these devices worked.

Bob's eyes widened. "We can negotiate, okay?" he said. "You want that kid's debt forgiven? Fine. You want more money next time? We can do that, too."

"I want you to stop being an asshole," I said, sorting

through the boxes along the counter until I found a small canister of black pigment. "But I realize that's hard to do, since being an asshole gets baked into your personality from a young age. So, I'm going to give you something that'll help."

Bob screamed and thrashed, and I had to stand behind the chair and put him in a headlock to keep him still long enough to do my work. His wide forehead made for a nice canvas, and the tattoo gun was well-maintained, but I must admit trying to write upside-down made for some shaky lettering.

I left Bob duct-taped to the seat, screaming himself hoarse, with a bandage over the new tattoo above his eyes. The Lube King and Goth Queen would never return, but whoever finally entered the Tat Cat would help Bob peel away the bandage to reveal 'LOZER' tattooed in enormous black letters. Imagine trying to engage in any kind of criminal activity with that mark.

I headed back to my apartment, ready to ride out the storm with my wine and snack food. That was when I received the text about Fiona, along with a link to a very peculiar app.

12

"WAIT," FIONA SAID. "What fucking app?"

We stood on a subway platform three stations away from where I'd saved their drenched asses from a squad of very serious folks. I was reasonably sure we were safe, at least for the moment. I'd thrown a few smoke grenades to cover our escape, forcing our pursuers to either give up or take their sweet time working their way through the tunnel system.

I pulled out my phone, flicked it to life, and tilted the screen to reveal the app's home-screen, which featured a number in a green box above a few lines of text. I scrolled up slightly to the header image: Fiona standing in a luxury kitchen, her mask pulled down and a handful of noodles in her hand. The shot was low-res black and white, and her face was a mess of pixels, but you never forget the woman who shot you in the back and almost severed your spine.

"What the hell?" Fiona asked.

"I guess wherever this was taken, they had a security camera," I said. "Maybe afraid the cook would try to steal a steak, a little five-finger discount."

"That paranoid billionaire fuck," Fiona said. "What's this app?"

I flicked left, revealing dozens of hyperlinked titles, each with either a little green or red number ticking alongside it:

LAMBO NEAR HIGH LINE: STEAL BACK
Would appreciate someone taking back my 'goods'
MAN IN GRAND CENTRAL: BREAK NOSE
GiMmE ReVenGe, PayInG ToP DolLar

One look at this overcrowded, throbbing interface would have made Steve Jobs's head explode. "It's called Dispatch," I said. "Not something you can download direct from the App Store. Invite-only. You want something bad done, you put it up on here, and you hope someone accepts whatever you're bidding."

"So, Craigslist for evil shit?" said the boy named Fireball, who leaned against the nearest wall, the girl named Jen hanging off his shoulder. The joke made her grin.

"Got it in one," I said, offering him a cheerful finger-gun. "Payment is in the cryptocurrency of your choice, for obvious reasons."

"An app," Fiona said, as if she couldn't believe it. "This is entrapment city."

"I assure you it's not," I said. "You can't get on it unless you're vetted. I don't even know who the webmaster is." Returning the phone to my pocket, I added, "Now, under ordinary circumstances, the price of the job dips the longer it stays up there. Encourages a hitter to take the job as fast as possible. But you? You're the prize of the night, because your number's barely going down at all. Whoever runs this app, they were persuaded to make you a special case."

"How much are we worth?" Fiona said. "The number on that screen was... ten?"

"Ten Bitcoin," I said. "You could buy ten of those fancy Tesla cars with that."

"With all the options," Fireball said, sounding almost excited.

"Any name for who put this contract on us?" Fiona asked. Her hand had rested on her weapon ever since we first met in the tunnel, and for good reason, I supposed. For all she knew, I was still sore about what happened in Oklahoma. I was waiting for her to ask how I'd managed to miraculously survive our little misunderstanding, but she seemed curiously uncurious. Maybe supposedly-dead assassins showing up to save her ass from other gunmen was a regular occurrence in her life.

"I got no idea who thinks you're worth that much," I said. "And I'm not going to hurt you, okay? You can ease off the gun."

"Why are you here?" she asked.

"Finally. I've been waiting for that question. Curiosity, I guess? Nothing good on Netflix tonight? What's with that jacket? You delivering food as a side hustle?"

"Part of a ruse," Fiona said, her hand lingering on the weapon. It made me wonder whether I was a little crazy to save someone who clearly wouldn't mind me dying again.

"It's really fashion-forward," I said. "I like it."

"Says the dude who once dressed up in an Elvis jumpsuit."

"Hey, it fit the moment."

"Explain to me again how you know each other?" asked Jen, her eyes yo-yoing between me and Fiona.

"Fiona's husband Bill once came up with the brilliant idea of stealing a couple million from his employers," I said. "Those employers happened to be a really nasty gang, though, and they tracked Bill down to Oklahoma—or rather, I tracked Bill down. Fiona was there, too, and we all ended up in a shootout with a bunch of rednecks who wanted the money. That about sum it up?"

"More or less," Fiona said.

"How'd you find us now?" Fireball asked me. "We only left that penthouse, like, an hour ago."

"Like I said, when it comes to tracking people, the only thing better's a hound dog," I said. "We need to go."

"We were already heading somewhere," Fiona said.

"Yeah, you were making real good progress, too, right up until I found you," I said.

"Bill's there," she said. "He might actually like to see you."

I'd liked Bill for the brief time I'd known him. If he could refrain from pickpocketing me, I felt we'd get along well. "Where?" I asked.

"Townhouse, twenty-third," she said. "Easy walk from here in normal conditions." Her eyes flicked to the ceiling.

"This is the same station I came in," I said, ejecting the half-full magazine from my rifle and reloading with a full one. "I got a truck right across the street. Unless Manhattan's under four feet of water, we'll make it. Let's go."

"Thank you," Jen said.

"You're very welcome, little lady," I said, offering my sunniest smile. "Always happy to help out a friend."

"Do you actually have a name?" she asked.

"Whatever he tells you, it'll be a lie," Fiona said.

"I've evolved past names, anyway," I offered, ignoring how Fiona rolled her eyes.

The wind roared down the short hallway connecting the station to the surface, toying with our hair. It sounded less like weather than an animal, a huge wolf threatening bloody doom. We exited through the emergency door and took a left beyond the stationmaster's kiosk, where we had a better view of the subway entrance. A waterfall poured down the steps into the bubbling gutter-strip that ran along the gate.

The rain had picked up since I went underground. If you went outside and lay on your back, you'd drown in a few seconds. I shrugged off my black nylon shell and draped it over Jen's shoulders. "It probably won't help," I said, "but it's better than nothing."

"Thanks," she said.

Slinging the submachine gun over my shoulder, I walked to the gate, which I'd pushed closed after snipping the lock. I forced it open again, the wind snapping at my ears, the rain needling my eyes. My shoes instantly soaked again.

"We might want to run," I told them, and, gripping the railing, pushed my way up the stairs. It was like fording whitewater, exhausting after even a few steps. At the top, I crouched and extended my hand to Fiona, who took it and pulled herself to the final step, then spun to help me with the kids.

Once everyone was topside, we paused to breathe. A crumpled highway sign bounced like razor-sharp tumbleweed down the middle of the street, denting a car door as it passed.

"Not something you see every day," Fiona said.

"My ride's there," I said, pointing across the street to the white blur of a truck parked at the corner. "We can make it, right? We're not wimps about a little weather?"

"Let's go," Fiona said, shoving past me. She had Jen tucked under her shoulder like a mama bird, trying to shield her from the storm, but her body proved as effective against the elements as a screen door on a submarine. Despite her warmth and my jacket, the kid was already shivering again. At least the city's electricity was still on, so I could fumble out my keys by the streetlights' sickly yellow glow.

I unlocked the truck, and we wrestled the doors open. In the back seat, Fiona and Jen slammed atop a geologic layer of burger wrappers and junk mail. Fireball plopped into the front passenger seat and, after shaking himself like a dog, opened his waterproof backpack and pulled out a laptop. Flipping the computer open, he stabbed the power button.

"What the hell are you doing?" I asked him. "Sending an email?"

"Gotta check if it still works," he said, breathless.

"Not our biggest problem," I said, twisting the engine to life while smacking buttons on the ancient dashboard until heat blasted from the vents.

"There a blanket or something back here?" Fiona asked.

"Sure, but you might have to excavate," I said, wiping the thin layer of condensation from the driver's side window so I could check the subway entrance. The was zero chance our pursuers could have tracked us to the subway station so quickly, but this was a night for odd events.

"Got it," Fiona said, yanking a ratty woolen blanket from beneath a stack of books in the footwell. "God, you ever think about cleaning this thing up?"

"Bring it up with the guy I stole it from," I said, twisting the wheel so I could edge us from the curb. The tires skidded against the rushing water. I was just as concerned about flying debris shattering the windshield.

Fiona wrapped the blanket around Jen, turning her into a wool burrito, before pulling her phone from her pocket and dialing.

"Who you calling?" I asked.

"Bill," she said, holding the phone to her ear.

"How's he doing?" I asked.

"Still Bill, and he's not picking up." Pulling the phone from her ear, she typed out a text.

"I'm sure he's okay," I said. "You mind telling me where we're going?"

"Head east," she said. "I'll tell you when to turn."

She dialed a number and placed the phone to her ear again.

"I'm sure he's okay," I said again.

"He's supposed to leave his phone on," she said. "And if I have signal, he probably has signal."

I almost told her it wasn't true. On a night like this, the usual rules never applied. Something in her face persuaded me to shut my mouth. Knowing Bill, he would have kept his phone on for Fiona. If he wasn't picking up, he might have become another problem for us to solve.

13

BILL TAPPED HIS pinkie fingers along the edges of the handcuffs. Easy to pick, if only he had the proper tools and a little privacy. The storm was making these cops nervous, and a nervous cop was like a wounded animal—quick to snap.

His wrist buzzed.

As someone who considered himself a connoisseur of fine timepieces—he'd stolen his first iced-out Rolex at nineteen— he had despised the idea of a computer on his wrist. *I'm not a nerd*, he told Fiona when she first mentioned buying one. A real watch was a useful tool of his trade. A chump, observing the equivalent of a new sports car on your left wrist, would assume you had a great deal of money, and trust you faster.

Oh, come on, Fiona retorted. *It's sleek, and you can get all kinds of shiny accessories for it.* A week later, she presented a smartwatch as a gift, along with a few straps in patent leather with gold buckles, sold not by the company that made the watch but a small leather shop down in the Village.

Of course, he knew why she wanted him to wear it. Fiona, who enjoyed starting her day with a hundred push-ups and sit-ups, who ran ten miles at a stretch to clear her head, wanted him to be healthier. In addition to telling time, the watch had health apps tracking everything from your heart rate to how many steps you took in a day. It had a cellular connection, so even if you left your phone at home, you could still take walks and record your route and even make a phone call—not that he would be caught dead shouting into his wrist in the middle of the street.

Well, someone was calling him now.

He should have tried dialing Fiona from the cops' car trunk. In his fear and confusion, he'd forgotten all about the feature. Anyway, what would he have told her? *I'm in a car but I don't know where?* He didn't even know where he was right now.

The cops had retreated to the table in the middle of the space, their heads bent together as they muttered through logistics. They would take the watch if they realized he could call or text with it. He needed some space.

"Hey," he called out.

The cops raised their heads as one. No sympathy in those gazes.

"I need to piss," he said.

His wrist buzzed twice: incoming text.

"Should let you go in your pants, sweetheart," said Tattoo.

"Come on," Bill said. "Just a bucket and thirty seconds."

The cops looked at Katzen.

"What?" Katzen said. "I'm not doing it."

"You brought him here," Crew Cut said, "which means you're the one pulling out his dick, okay? Small price to pay for how badly you fucked up."

"I didn't fuck up," Katzen said, his cheeks reddening. "We agreed to the plan. We carried out the plan. How was I supposed to know the guy was out of town?"

"You're the fancy homicide detective," Tattoo snorted. "That's your job, to find out."

Katzen looked at Hardaway, his eyes begging for backup, but she only shrugged. "Just do it," she said. "We don't have time for this shit."

Katzen made a show of slapping the table and puffing out his cheeks. It didn't matter. The other cops had him pegged. Bill had him pegged, too. Katzen was the chump.

"Fine," Katzen said, retrieving an empty five-gallon bucket from the corner and marching over to Bill.

"I appreciate it," Bill said. "You're a great guy."

"Shut up," Katzen said, dumping the bucket on the floor between Bill's spread legs.

Bill offered the cop a look of wide-eyed innocence. "If you unzip me, I can kind of bump my hips, let it flop out. You won't even have to touch it. Will that work for you?"

Muffled chuckling from the table. "Yeah, Katzen," Crew Cut shouted. "Will that work for you?"

"I'll just uncuff you," Katzen said. "You try anything, I'll kill you. Understood?"

"You're the boss," Bill said.

Katzen moved behind Bill's chair. Bill felt the cop's hands brush his wrists, pull at the chain connecting the handcuffs.

Bill's watch buzzed again.

Katzen paused. Had he felt the vibration?

"Bladder's full," Bill almost shouted.

"What was that?" Katzen asked.

"What was what?"

"That sound."

"Your phone?" Bill said. "Come on, man."

Katzen patted his jacket. "Not my phone."

"Well, you took mine." Bill's heart pounded against his sternum.

Katzen paused for what felt like an infinity. If he saw the smartwatch, would he know it came with a cellular connection? You could tell it had the feature because of the red dot on the bezel, but Katzen didn't strike Bill as the type who paid much attention to technology.

Click, click, and the metal bracelets snapped open. Bill rubbed his wrists and stood on cracking knees. With his right foot, he pushed the bucket away from the chair, then pivoted so he stood above it, his back to the table and its assembled cops. Katzen was still in front of him, posing a problem.

"You want to compare sizes?" Bill asked, unzipping his pants.

"You ever been to jail?" Katzen smirked. "I bet you have. No privacy."

Bill shrugged, unzipped, and pulled out what the most immature part of his brain still referred to as the one-eyed love worm. After drinking so much wine earlier, he really did need to piss enough to refill a reservoir. He felt blessed relief as his stream splashed into the bottom of the bucket.

Katzen shifted his gaze.

Bill swiveled on his heel, arcing his piss beyond the bucket and onto the cop's shoes. Katzen yelped and jumped back. Bill grinned and swiveled again, chasing him with his yellow stream. Behind them, the other cops roared laugher.

"Privacy," Bill said.

"Fuck you," Katzen snapped, shaking the urine from his shoes as he hopped out of Bill's sight. An hour ago, Bill might have feared Katzen shooting him the back of the head, but he had the cop's number now. The guy was a beta dog.

Bill aimed at the bucket again. Trying to move as quickly but subtly as he could, he used his right thumb to push back his left sleeve, exposing his fancy smartwatch. Touching the bezel brought the device to life, and he tapped the screen until the app icons popped into view. Tapped the message icon. Fiona had texted him: *Where U?*

She was alive and hunting for him. Excellent. Best news of a crappy night. His bladder was almost empty, his flow slackening, but he only needed another few seconds. He tapped the microphone icon below Fiona's last message, and a gray line wiggled across the screen as the smartwatch's microphone snapped to life.

"You done, prick?" Katzen asked.

"You speaking to my disco stick, or to me?" Bill said, shaking out the last drops, which had the nice side effect of dropping his left sleeve over his wrist again. He shoved himself into his pants and zipped up.

"I'm not even dignifying that with a response," Katzen said. "Sit back down and put your hands behind your back, perp."

"Oh, perp. You know how to really hurt a guy's feelings." Bill sat, using his right foot to push the piss bucket a few inches further away from him.

As Katzen knelt behind him with the handcuffs, Bill said, "So, you've kidnapped me, dragged me to this police garage or whatever it is on the West Side, somewhere near Midtown, and next we're going to North Brother Island? Quite an adventure."

"Shut up," Katzen said, snapping the handcuffs onto Bill's wrists, the metal biting into his skin. "I don't care."

"You ought to. You're a cop," Bill said. "You're all cops. You took an oath to uphold the law, right?"

"Shut up," Katzen said, walking away. "It'll go easier on you if you shut the fuck up."

Leaning back in his seat, Bill bent his wrists so the fingers of his right hand slipped beneath his left sleeve. Whenever you composed a message on the smartwatch, you finished by tapping the Send icon in the screen's upper-right corner, correct?

He tapped that area repeatedly, hoping the message sent— And now what?

He hadn't offered up an exact address. And even if he could—what did he expect Fiona to do, crash through the hurricane to rescue him? The roof banged like Thor himself was slamming his hammer into the metal. Moving more than a few blocks was suicidal.

At least she would know he was kidnapped.

The lights flickered.

Crew Cut retrieved a paper from Bill's folder and walked over. Standing over Bill, he rolled the paper into a tube, crinkling it in his grip. A nervous gesture. His eyes cold and unblinking.

"You're not bullshitting us about this island?" Crew Cut asked.

Bill shook his head. "No."

"Good. We're not bad guys. We're going to cut you in. It's in your interest to tell us everything you know."

"Just to make sure everything runs smoothly?"

"Correct." Crew Cut offered him a tight-lipped smile. "Now you're getting it."

"You know what I know," Bill said, nodding at the paper. "It's all in there."

"There's nothing you're holding back, just in case?"

"Look, I don't know what that could be. We might have to dig in a few places."

"We'll be the judge of that." Crew Cut snapped.

"Sorry." Bill made a show of averting his gaze, every inch the cowed criminal. "I'll follow your lead."

"Good. We're not bad guys. Everyone's getting well at the end of this." Crew Cut turned away, about to return to the table.

"Why are you doing this?" Bill said. "The hedge fund guy was your original plan. Now the island. Not without risk. I thought you cops had good pensions."

"Oh, the pension's fine." Crew Cut regarded the other cops, who were doing a great job of not looking up from whatever occupied them around the table. No doubt they were listening. "But you always need something more. You know how it goes."

"Sure," Bill said. "Sure, I do."

"Besides, being a cop isn't what it used to be. When I first started out, cops got respect. Even the worst criminals, the true thugs, they gave it to us, because they knew the consequences if they didn't. Now it's all changed. You can't even search someone without a bunch of progressive vegans trying to shove a bunch of lawyers right up your ass. We're trying to do our jobs, keep the streets safe, and they're protesting us."

Oh no, Bill thought. He's on a roll.

Crew Cut's cheeks reddened. "Imagine putting your life on the line every day to protect this city, and all you get for it is people spitting in your face. Even my daughter, she's walking around the house shouting things like, 'Defund the police.' Excuse me, but if we walked off the job, it'd just be chaos. Everything would shut down."

"Sure," Bill said. "The blood-dimmed tide down Fifth Avenue."

"You can joke all you want, but you know it's true. We're the only line of defense against the animals. But if people can't appreciate that, I'm fine with taking my money and walking away from it all." His voice rose. "Isn't that right, everyone?"

Grunts of agreement from around the table.

"Thank you for illuminating me," Bill said. "I mean it. I might be a criminal, but I've always had respect for cops. You're just trying to do your job."

"Thank you," Crew Cut said, his tone flat. "I appreciate it. Even if I do have you cuffed up in a shithole on Tenth."

Crew Cut returned to the table. The garage doors rattled, the wind whistling through the joints and cracks. As Bill imagined cars spinning down the streets like poker chips, he ran his fingers over the edges of the smartwatch. Thanks to Crew Cut's slip of the tongue, he knew a little more about his location. Another text to Fiona, and she might have enough data to save his ass after all.

14

THE TRUCK RUMBLED down 23rd Street. At least, Fiona hoped they were on 23rd Street. The water smashing into the windshield reduced visibility to squat. The assassin hunched over the wheel, squinting into the blur, barely fluttering the gas as they crept forward.

At least the street was narrow, lined with secondhand jewelry stores and seedy bodegas shuttered against the storm. It blocked some of the wind slicing from the south. Hopefully protected them from some of the debris, too. Fiona feared a crashed or double-parked car in their way.

In the back seat, Fireball sat with his arm around Jen, pressing her close to transfer his body heat. Fireball had volunteered to change seats with Fiona, a sweet gesture, but everyone needed to change out of these wet clothes before hypothermia set in. A little bit of food and a bottle of wine wouldn't hurt, either. With food in her belly and alcohol in her bloodstream, Fiona could think a little more clearly about their savage dilemma.

They were at serious risk. But what else was new?

The truck must have descended into a shallow dip of some sort, almost too gentle to notice, because water crashed over the hood, splashing the windshield muddy. The engine whining. The assassin hissing through his teeth as he pushed the gas harder. He glanced at her, and she resisted the urge to touch her gun.

Fiona considered herself something of an academic in the specialized field of fatal gunshot wounds, and when she'd shot this dude in the middle of an Oklahoma field, she was one hundred percent certain her bullet had snapped his spine and ruptured enough organs to send him to the morgue— and yet here he was, alive and well enough to drive through a hurricane.

"You're thinking too much," he said.

"Never heard that one before."

"You almost killed me," the assassin said. "Hell, I was so close to the pearly gates, I was ready for the King himself to come out and welcome me home with a bitchin' guitar solo."

"What?"

"I probably did die, for a minute or two. Then I got better." The assassin grinned. "Spent some time in a hospital, before the FBI persuaded me to move on."

"Shouldn't you focus on the road?"

"I am focused. Don't worry, you'll like this part: I stole a serial killer's car." The assassin chuckled. "Can you believe it? All the cars in Oklahoma, I hijack the one belonging to a multiple murderer. Things got a little interesting after that, let's say. But I made it through. Made it back."

"And now what?"

The assassin shrugged. "Damned if I know. I was breaking folks' kneecaps for a couple of months in there, but that isn't the most spiritually fulfilling line of work, if you know what I mean?"

Fireball piped up from the back: "What did you charge?"

The assassin met the kid's eyes in the rearview mirror. "Why? You want a deal on someone? I got a good Friday special, two kneecaps for the price of one."

Fireball giggled. "You know, there's this one asshole in my 'Call of Duty' group…"

"Cut it out," Fiona said. "What are you hoping to get out of this?"

"This?"

"Us. Rescuing us."

The assassin shrugged. "Had nothing better to do."

"Bullshit."

"Take it as you will."

Fiona's phone buzzed. She snatched it from her pocket, the screen bright with a new text from Bill: *Prick disco stick hurt my feelings so you can help me drive me to this warehouse on the west side of next north brother island quiet adventure.*

"Who's that?" Fireball asked.

"Bill," Fiona said, her heart leaping. What the hell was this text? What warehouse? Where on the West Side? And what was the next North Brother Island quiet adventure?

"Is he dictating or quoting Lady Gaga lyrics?" Fireball said, jutting his head between the seats for a better look at the screen.

"Ha, you're so fucking funny," Fiona said. "Why is he outside in this shit?"

"Your husband's got poor impulse control," the assassin offered.

"Thank you for the most obvious statement of the century," Fiona said.

"What's North Brother Island?" Jen asked. She was still shivering despite the blanket and Fireball's body. She needed dry clothes and an entertaining movie on television, Fiona decided. Anything to help blot out whatever horrors she had endured in that penthouse.

"It's in Long Island Sound. Nothing's on it," Fiona said. Except Bill had a theory about a lot of money buried in its cursed soil, courtesy of their former boss. But who would Bill share that information with?

The answer was nobody, of course. Not unless someone forced him.

"Maybe he was kidnapped," Fireball said.

"Wouldn't be the first time," she said.

They crossed Fifth Avenue, which had become more of a rushing river than a street. Hurricane winds blasting down four empty lanes with enough force to send raindrops slithering up her window. The lightning constant, millions of volts razoring from the sky to slice roofs and trees. The engine bucking and grinding now, the dashboard lights flickering, maybe too much water sluicing through circuits and engine parts.

"Next block, park midway up it," Fiona told the assassin. "North side of the street."

The universe afforded them the small mercy of a parking space not too far from the front door of the townhouse. "Kill the engine," she said once they parked. "We're going in fast and quiet. Fireball, you and Jen stay in the car until we clear."

The engine died with a sick rattle. The assassin patted the dashboard. "I'd say that's sayonara for this sweet baby."

"Last ride's the greatest," Fiona said, ejecting the magazine from her pistol for a shell count. Enough ammunition to handle an attacker or three, but if there was a squad up there, she would retreat. The narrow stairwell leading from the front door to the living room was a kill box she needed to sprint through. Plenty of cover in the living room.

"I don't really do quiet," the assassin said, retrieving his antique submachine gun. "But blasting the shit out of people, I got that part down pat."

Fiona opened her door and the rain was a cold bucket right in the face, and she screamed to motivate herself as she slipped out, staying low as she circled around the rear of the car. The assassin already on the sidewalk, closing his door behind him.

The door operated via a four-digit code punched into a pad beside the lock. If anyone was in the kitchen or living room, they would hear the beeps. Crouched in the vestibule, she waited with her hand on the keypad until thunder boomed overhead, then punched in the code.

The lock clicked.

She shouldered the door open. Pistol up.

Quick, quick, quick up the stairwell into the living room. Sweep left and right. No targets. She crouched behind the couch, listening, waiting. Still nothing.

The place was empty.

Someone had ransacked it, though. Books and papers and food everywhere. Raising a hand for the assassin to stay in place, she swept into the first bedroom, the office, the bathroom: empty, ransacked. The second and third bedrooms: empty, ransacked. Through the windows, illuminated by the flicker-flash of lightning, she saw the terrace flooded with a few inches of water, the branches of its pretty tree flailing against the brick.

"Clear," she called from the first bedroom, where she stripped off her wet shirt and bra, along with that damn Wok the Line jacket, and slipped on a black t-shirt. The dry cloth felt amazing against her skin. She pulled a few of Bill's t-shirts off a nearby table before returning to the kitchen, where the assassin had set his weapon atop the island and helped himself to the assortment of luxury bites. She was about to criticize him before thinking better of it—they could all use the calories.

"Who do you think tossed the joint?" he asked between swallows.

"No clue," she said. No blood on the floor or teeth in the sink. Whatever happened to Bill, at least he hadn't been hurt.

Hurt in here, the demon whispered in her head. *They could have taken him some other place. They could be torturing the shit out of him right now.*

Best not to think of such things.

"Here," she said, tossing the assassin one of Bill's t-shirts. It was blue, with an oversized Superman logo on the front.

"Great, I can disguise myself as a nerd," the assassin said, stripping off his wet top, revealing a torso etched with purple scars. The freshest was bright red and maybe three inches long, tracing to the left of his belly button. A souvenir of Fiona's bullet.

"You know you love it," Fiona said, tempted to say something more, really drill into that night in Oklahoma, but she was saved by footsteps on the stairs. Fireball appeared, still with his arm around Jen. "You weren't going to just leave us down there, were you?" he snapped.

"We had to clear," Fiona said.

"Come on," Fireball told Jen, escorting her to the closest leather couch in the living room. Once she was seated, he plucked the bearskin rug off the floor and draped it around her shoulders. She sagged under the weight but smiled at him.

"What now, chief?" the assassin asked Fiona.

"I don't know," she said. "Bill's phone's not here, so whatever happened, I presume it's with him."

"Or whoever took him," Fireball said, plucking two wool blankets from a nearby leather chair and tossing one over Jen's legs. Next, he stripped off his wet shirt—revealing a line of small tattoos running up his ribs, runes of some sort—and wrapped himself in the second blanket.

"Here," Fiona said, tossing the kids a pair of t-shirts before opening the fridge. Bill loved the good stuff, the wines with impossible-to-pronounce names that cost hundreds of dollars per bottle, but what she wanted most in the world right now was a beer, cheap and delicious and cool on her aching throat.

"You and Bill have the same phone account?" Fireball asked, dropping the blanket and slipping on the t-shirt. "Same password and everything?"

"Yeah?" Fiona shut the fridge door without retrieving a beer, more interested in whatever Fireball was trying to tell her.

"Then you can use that 'Find My Device' feature, you know?" Fireball said. "The one that shows where your devices are on a map?"

"Hey, I like this kid," the assassin said.

"Set it up," Fiona said.

Fireball peeled open his backpack and extracted the laptop. Flipping it open, the screen's ghostly light playing across his face, he began typing. "It's quick, just a website," he said. "Come over here and log in."

He placed the laptop on the coffee table, the screen facing

her. She recognized her phone service's website. She knelt and typed her username and password into the appropriate box. A map of New York City popped up, along with icons of all the devices linked to their account, including Bill's smartwatch.

She clicked on the smartwatch icon, and a bright blue dot sprang into existence on the West Side, somewhere north of the Javits Center. There were a lot of warehouses and chop shops over there, but also a lot of luxury condos, gleaming skyscrapers. Had they taken Bill to one of the latter? The prospect of having to assault two ultra-rich high-rises in one night was funny, an incredible cosmic fuckup. She giggled.

"What's so funny?" the assassin asked.

"Absolutely nothing," she said, clicking to the map's satellite view and zooming in until the outlines of buildings appeared. The blue dot wasn't centered on high-rise but a flat, block-wide building. A warehouse or a vehicle depot. A concrete box with few or no windows, making it nicely storm-resistant. An address materialized beside the blue dot. She copied it, about to paste it into a search engine, when the dot disappeared.

"It's gone," she said.

Fireball peered over her shoulder. "Signal cut."

"From the storm?"

"Maybe." Fireball shrugged. "Either that, or they found it."

"We should go," Fiona said, already thinking through logistics, what and who to take. Her bones felt heavy as lead. Her muscles like water. It was so cold and wet and dangerous out there, and she felt so small and weak. How much more violence tonight? How many bodies—

"Go out in this?" Fireball stepped away from the laptop,

raising his hands. "No way. No way am I going out in this crap again..."

"Not you," Fiona said, logging out of the website, opening a new browser tab, and pasting in the address. The first couple of hits offered squat, but the other links on the page led to city government websites, PDFs referring to the address as an "NYPD storage facility." Wonderful. Had Bill been kidnapped by cops?

If so, it wouldn't be the first time. The universe was laughing at them, wasn't it?

"Kid has a point," the assassin said. "It's only getting messier out there. And the truck's fucked."

"I know," she said. Returning to the kitchen island, she tore off a hunk of bread and loaded it with some of the fine meats Bill had purchased with the millionaire's stolen credit card. "But I have a crazy idea about how to get from Point A to B."

15

FIONA WAS SUSPICIOUS of my intentions.

And why not? She'd shot me in the back. I'd be well within my rights to hold a bit of a grudge.

Except I didn't.

Granted, if you'd shot me in the back a few years ago, and I miraculously survived, I would have devoted a stunning amount of time, energy, blood, and brainpower to ensuring whatever I left of you could fit into a small cardboard box. But I'd sworn to avoid killing as much as possible, and unlike yoga, drinking, and ridding my diet of all carbohydrates, it was one promise I intended to stick to.

I also took no offense when Fiona kept one hand on the pistol in her belt as she conducted our happy crew into the deeper regions of this weird house. She tried to make it look casual, like she always walked around with one hand on her hip, but I'd been doing this long enough to know better. She must have known I knew it, too.

We entered a small office off the second bedroom. Its lone window overlooked the terrace. A desk carved from a heavily lacquered log dominated half the space. On it rested a top-of-the-line Mac monitor in bright blue, beside a gold bust of eternal warrior-poet Tupac Shakur. The owner of this place had committed the ultimate act of sacrilege by fitting a headset with a built-in mic onto Tupac's ears, as if the rapper had been reduced to working in a call center.

"I heard Tupac's living with Elvis in Cuba," I said, pointing at the bust. "They smoke a couple of those nice Cohiba cigars every afternoon before heading down to the local restaurant for the octopus special."

"Who's Tupac?" Jen asked.

Behind the desk, on the back of the ergonomic office chair that cost more than my rent, was a folded-up sweatshirt I picked up and tossed at Jen. "You mean you don't recognize the second-best rapper to ever work the mic?" I asked her.

"You mean Drake? That looks nothing like Drake," Fireball said, smirking because he knew he was messing with me, and because he didn't know I could have killed him with a No. 2 pencil.

"They are not teaching the right things in schools these days," I said. Removing the headset, I hefted the bust by the jaw, surprised by the weight. "Feels like a lot of gold."

"Sorry to bust your bubble, but Bill thinks it's almost all lead," Fiona said, opening one of the cabinets lining the walls. On a rack inside hung twenty suits, exquisitely tailored. She shoved the suits aside, revealing the closet's wooden back, which featured a small bronze hole in the center.

"Let me guess," I said. "Is it the world's most micro-sized glory hole?"

"It's a keyhole. For a key we couldn't find." Fiona pointed to the upper-left corner of the panel, which featured a deep gash. "Couple swings with a hammer, Bill figured out it's solid metal behind there. No smashing through."

Fireball squinted into the hole. "I bet I could figure it out. No disrespect to Bill, but lockpicking was my hobby for a bunch of years. Sometimes with these trick locks, it's not just a matter of finding the right key—you also need to depress a small button somewhere nearby to open a panel blocking the rest of the channel. I also once saw this lock that had, like, indents instead of pins, it's hard to describe…"

I was getting bored.

Fireball sidestepped to the desk, opened its top drawer, and fetched two paperclips. Straightening the clips, he returned to the lock. "Something like this, the other issue is the shear line might not be normal—it's what bisects the driver and key pins—or there might be multiple ones, which can lead to a weird conundrum when…"

"How long is this going to take?" Fiona said.

Fireball shrugged. "Hours, unfortunately. You really have to make friends with a lock, right? Put your ear right up to it so it can speak to you…"

"Stand back," I said.

"What?" Fireball shot me an irritated look. "You saying you have better skills than me?"

"Nope." In one smooth motion, I hoisted the Tupac bust. "I got a Rap God."

As Fireball scrambled away, I lifted the bust over my head, grunting between clenched teeth, and hurled it as hard as I could at the lock. The Rap God's forehead smashed a bowl-shaped divot in the panel before tumbling to the carpet, the lock's crushed bits raining down.

The panel creaked open, revealing a cabinet with three wooden shelves.

Fireball stared at me in awe. "How did you know that would work?"

"Ever hear of the Gordian knot?" I said.

Fiona pulled out the top drawer, revealing twelve enormous timepieces set in velvet nests. Each of the watches glittered with diamonds and other precious metals. I guessed they were worth fifty thousand dollars apiece, easily, and they were all heavy enough to drag you straight to the bottom of a river if you were unfortunate enough to tumble in while wearing one.

"Fireball," Fiona said, "go in the next room and find me a bag." Shutting the top drawer, she opened the next one down, revealing small bags filled with white powder and pills and weed, along with small gold coins with ancient symbols on them. Closing that drawer, she opened last one: legal documents, including a last will.

Fireball returned with a nylon sack. Fiona dumped the watches into it, followed by the drugs and gold coins. "Got to be worth a quarter-million, no?"

"What exactly are you thinking?" I asked.

"I'm going to call Boz." She hefted the bag, testing its weight. "He's the guy who set me up with that assignment. He's got an RV that's 'hurricane-proof,' or so he said. He'll give us a ride, I think, for a price."

"Expensive taxi," I said.

"Well, the penthouse job went bad. He told me to pay him twenty grand by tomorrow or he'd kill me. I figure this will make us good."

Fireball and Jen stared at her as if she'd sprouted two heads. "What?" she snapped at them. "It'll work."

"What about the app?" Fireball asked.

Fiona pointed at me. "What's the price on us?"

I pulled out my phone and flicked the app open. In my head, I converted the displayed Bitcoin to dollars, which came to a number with many zeroes after it. I almost made a joke about collecting the money myself.

"Pretty high," I said. Understatement of the century.

"Well, maybe we can reach an understanding," she said, which I knew was Fiona-speak for killing everyone if they so much as blinked the wrong way.

"Maybe."

"Go in the living room," she pulled out her phone. "I want to make this call."

With the Tupac bust under my arm, I escorted the kids to the front of the house, wondering in my usual paranoia why Fiona needed the privacy. Was she going to sell me out? If so, why? I was useless to pretty much anybody. Once upon a time, the Rockaway Mob might have offered a princely sum for my head in a box, but all those morons were dead.

In the kitchen, I set the bust on the island and asked the kids, "You have any dietary issues? I know a lot of you do these days."

"I'm just allergic to bullshit," Jen said, grinning again.

"Excellent," I said, picking through the packages of food. Bill had really splurged, hadn't he? My rumbling stomach demanded I create the Mother of All Sandwiches. Snatching the sharpest-looking breadknife from the block, I sliced a baguette open and loaded it with a couple thousand calories' worth of meats and cheeses. I was going to bake this fucker up in the oven and sprinkle it with a variety of herbs—such a finely appointed place must have an herb rack, no?

"Are we coming with you?" Fireball squeaked. "I'm not sure how useful I could be."

"Maybe if we need a bullet sponge," I told him as I worked. "But fortunately for you, I don't think we do. You two are going to stay here."

Jen shook her head. "That's not going to work."

"Why not?" I asked.

"You're going to ask this scary dude to just drive right up to the front door? You drive away, someone comes in and grabs us."

"Good tactical thinking," I said, twisting around to flip the oven knob to 400 degrees. "But I'm already ahead of you. We'll arrange for them to pick us up a little way away from here."

"They could still find out where we are," Fireball said.

"You're a bit of a sniveling coward, aren't you?" I asked. "Do either of you see any tinfoil around here?"

"Excuse me?" Fireball said. To the kid's credit, he tried puffing out his chest like a second-tier hood in a Van Damme action flick, as if he had a chance of beating me up on my worst day.

"Never mind, we'll go old-school." I retrieved a cookie sheet from a rack above the oven and slid the oversized sandwich onto it. "Kid, you're out of your depth here. Not your fault, exactly. But why don't you worry more about what *definitely* might kick your ass, and less about could *possibly* kick your ass, understand?"

Fireball squinted. "No?"

"Okay, fine." I slid the sandwich into the oven. Walked

over to the island and picked up the submachine gun, offering it to him. "I'm going to leave this for you. Know how to use it?"

"I've never shot a gun," Fireball said. "But I've played a lot of 'Battlefield.' Snap off the safety, pull the trigger?"

"Sure." My voice rose into a falsetto imitation of my little friend. "'Snap off the safety, pull the trigger.' Maybe you'll produce enough noise to scare the person running at you."

"Here." Jen stepped forward, waving her hand for the gun. "My foster father taught me to shoot. He even had old guns like this."

I handed her the weapon, curious if she could handle the weight. Despite her stick-arms and sickly disposition, she gripped the weapon with the studied skill of an Old West desperado. She was also smart enough to keep the barrel aimed away from us, her forefinger well away from the trigger.

"What's your story, little miss?" I asked her.

She shrugged and handed the weapon back. "Foster home. It sucked. And they sold me to whoever was going to take my kidneys. I know because my foster father bought a Corvette last week."

"I was a foster kid, too," I said, which wasn't exactly the truth. From what a bored administrator told me at one point, my alcoholic mother had left me locked in her crappy Datsun on a super-hot day. That must have given me some trust issues, because for the next sixteen years I bounced from institution to institution, not breaking any records academically but voted Most Likely to End Up on Death Row by a legion of counselors and supervisors. Every time they tried shipping me off to a foster family, it usually lasted a grand total of three hours before I either set something on fire or blew something up.

At least I never lost my world-famous sense of humor.

"I'm sorry," Jen said.

"Wasn't that bad. I got a lot of reading done in solitary," I offered, setting the submachine gun on the island. I felt a little better about leaving these kids alone—if the worst happened, I sensed Jen would lay down some accurate fire while Fireball did his best to squeeze beneath a couch. "Go check the fridge. There's probably something good to drink in there."

Fiona entered the kitchen, dressed now in black water-proof gear, loose pants tucked into hiking boots. Her pistol in a plastic holster on her hip. Her phone dangling from her left hand. She plucked a wad of meat from an open package and stuffed it in her mouth and chewed slowly, her eyes closed. I hoped she was ready for whatever awfulness lay ahead.

"What's the news?" Jen asked.

Fiona swallowed. "We're leaving in twenty," she said. "I arranged pick-up a few blocks from here."

"You afraid they'll shoot you in the back?" Fireball offered.

I patted Tupac's golden head. "Believe it or not, I have an idea for solving that part," I said. "But if you have another pistol, I'm gonna need it."

16

THE STORM HAD found a hole in the depot roof. What started as a slow drip maybe ten feet to Bill's left intensified into a miniature waterfall, a pool creeping toward him. Bill shifted his legs to the right, anxious to spare his shoes.

Crew Cut paced the rear of the warehouse, a phone pressed to his ear. It was difficult to hear his conversation over the hurricane's nonstop roar, but Bill figured he was talking about the logistics of a boat. The other cops clustered around the table, checking their phones. They had settled in for the long haul, piling their guns and jackets and half-empty snack bags and soda cans atop Bill's notes and the tools.

The closest weapon was Hardaway's Glock-19 in the shoulder holster she stripped off and hung on the back of her chair, but it was still a good twenty feet away—too far for Bill to reach without someone tackling or shooting him, even if he did pick the handcuff locks.

Tattoo fiddled with the knobs of a police radio, producing nothing but static except for the occasional burst of voices, loud and panicked and stuffed with cop jargon.

"Flooding at the stock exchange," Soul Patch said, flicking his phone screen.

"You got signal?" Hardaway said.

"Yeah, but it keeps going in and out." Soul Patch swiped again. "Coney Island's getting smashed."

"You mean, smashed in a different way than usual." Katzen chuckled at his own witticism.

"Hey." Soul Patch jabbed a finger. "I'm from there. You watch your mouth."

"All those folks drifting out to sea on a swell of crushed beer cans and needles," Katzen said. "It's a real tragedy."

Soul Patch rose from his seat, his right hand clenched into a fist. Katzen raised his hands, palms out, and said, "I'm sorry, man. Just trying to lighten the mood."

"Lighten this," Soul Patch said, grabbing his crotch as he sat down again.

"You know that big crane on top of that skyscraper off Fifth?" Tattoo said, tapping his screen. "Looks like the wind twisted it down. Gonna fall."

The lights flickered. The rasp of something heavy on the roof. Bill did some math: if they were on Ninth or Tenth, it was a few yards to the West Side Highway, which had four or six lanes—he couldn't remember. And beyond, the piers they used for tour boats and such. Not much elevation. If there was a storm surge of three or four feet, would it come far enough inland to flood this place?

A drop of water smacked the table, followed by another. The cops stood and backed off, cursing. From the far side of the depot, Crew Cut lowered the phone from his ear long enough to shout, "Just move it away, okay?"

While the cops shifted the table, Bill figured it was a good time to fiddle with his smartwatch. Press the bezel twice to open the app menu, then—well, there was no way he could tell the apps apart by feel. What happened if he pressed the little button beneath the bezel? It would open a screen of recent apps, including the messaging app he'd just used.

Okay, so if he pressed that button, then tapped the center of the screen, it would open the messaging app. What did that interface look like? Fiona's message was probably front-and-center. He would only need to tap again to activate it, then hit the little microphone button in the top-right. Give her a better idea of location...

His finger hovered over the button.

What would he say out loud? Another rant, of course. Mix in some details she can use. Number of cops. Vehicles. Anything.

He pressed the button—and a rough hand gripped his wrist, yanked it.

Bill yelped.

Crew Cut had snuck up behind him. With a low growl, the man snapped the smartwatch off Bill's wrist, dropped it on the concrete, and smashed it one, two, three times with the heel of his boot. The screen shattered, bits of electronics skittering everywhere.

"He was doing something," Crew Cut yelled to the other cops. "None of you fucking idiots check him for one of those things?"

"One of what?" Tattoo said, trotting over.

"Those watches with the screen," Crew Cut snapped,

giving the smartwatch another stomp for good measure. "He was touching it behind his back."

"I wasn't doing anything," Bill said, his heart pounding. "I swear."

"Bullshit." Crew Cut's rough hand on the back of Bill's neck, squeezing his spine. "Better tell us what you're up to, asshole. Right now. Or you're going to die."

"Would've been better if you hadn't smashed it," Katzen said, pulling Bill's phone from his pocket. Holding it high, he hit the power button so they could all see the lock screen, wallpapered with an iconic Man Ray photograph. No notifications. "I don't think he sent anything. There's no activity on this."

"What were you fucking doing?" Crew Cut said, leaning so close Bill could smell the coffee on his breath.

"Just fiddling," Bill said.

"Even if he sent a message, nobody's coming anyway," Tattoo said, jutting his chin at the rattling ceiling. "Not in this shit. Besides, Bill here wants his share of the loot, am I right?"

Tattoo winked at Bill as if they were pals sharing an inside joke. *They think I'm a moron*, Bill marveled. *These cops, they've spent so many years smashing dumbasses' heads into the pavement, they really believe every criminal they encounter has an I.Q. the same as their shoe size. They'll underestimate me, which is useful, unless one of them shoots me on impulse—*

Crew Cut stepped away and, reaching behind his back, drew a silver .38 from his waistband. Cocked the hammer back.

Katzen snapped: "We kill him here, we're leaving evidence in a police warehouse, *jackass*. You think of all the cameras in this neighborhood? Watching us drive in and out?"

"Shut your fucking mouth," Crew Cut growled back.

"Bomb," Bill said, staring at Crew Cut's forehead as if he could project a single thought into the cop's brain: *You shouldn't shoot me.*

Crew Cut cocked his head.

"The Dean," Bill said, the words rushing out. "He'd have figured that if they ever decided to turn the island into a theme park or a casino or yet another of those luxury condo complexes, they'd start by demolishing the buildings. He couldn't take the risk of a bunch of construction guys running off with his money."

The .38 lowered a fraction. "Bomb?"

"The Dean was paranoid. He liked booby traps. He's the only guy I've ever known to spend money on a fucking claymore mine, if you can believe it. You think he'd bury a lot of cash without making sure it'd be protected from anyone trying to get at it?"

"And?"

"I know how he thinks." Bill nodded. "Look, none of you wants to take this risk, and if I'm wrong, I'll just be the one who blows himself sky-high, okay? How's that sound? You need me."

You need me. A terrifying phrase. The final cry of traitors on their knees in the swamps beyond the runways at JFK. Would it be enough? Because if it wasn't, they would shoot him and throw his body to the storm, and Fiona would never find him—

If this is your last moment, concentrate on her. That first bedroom you shared together, the narrow one with the white linen curtains, where the light pouring through the windows early in the morning would soften the lines of her face and angle through her pupils in a way that turned her eyes to diamonds. Think about the warmth of her smooth skin pressed against yours, the smell of the nape of her neck when she pushed her hair up, the way she laughed and how you knew that laugh was evidence of the ultimate goodness of the universe, how all the atoms and cells and physics of ten billion years could smash together to create something so pure and good—

The pistol wavered. "What were you doing with your watch?" Crew Cut asked, quieter now.

"Nothing, I swear," Bill said. "When I'm anxious, I fiddle around."

On the table, the radio spat static, followed by a screech and a panicked cop yelling about flooding on the West Side Highway, need to divert, emergency—

A metallic rattle. The roll-up door to their right shuddered in its track as it rose, wind and water bursting through the widening gap. Headlights blazing across wet concrete. An engine revving loud.

Crew Cut pointed his pistol at the car barreling into the depot as the rest of the crew scrambled toward the table and their weapons.

Bill thought: *Baby! You're here!*

Except it wasn't Fiona. The depot lights revealed the car's roof flashers, the blue "NYPD" on the driver's side door—a cruiser with a smashed bumper and cracked windows, screeching to a stop. Two anxious cops peering at them through the windshield.

17

THIS WAS THE shittiest of shitty ideas, Fiona thought as she guided the assassin down 23rd Street in the wind and lashing rain. They stuck as close to the buildings as they could, setting their feet before taking the next step, like explorers grinding toward the top of Mount Everest with no oxygen in their tanks. She felt incredibly small in the face of this monstrosity tearing its way across the city, shredding even the largest buildings like toys.

"Just as long as it takes out Times Square," she muttered, and the assassin gave her a curious look.

Before leaving, they had stripped the closets of all top-end waterproof gear. Enclosed in layers of nylon and plastic and canvas, they made good progress, closing on the target intersection in time to witness a cloud of leaves and branches zipping up the avenue. The old church on the corner had a deep stone arch around its front door that provided miserable cover. It didn't protect them completely from the rain, but it spared them from the worst of the wind.

"I still don't get why you brought that big Tupac head," Fiona told the assassin. "Isn't it heavy?"

"You forgot one thing about Boz." The assassin chuckled, cradling the bright gold bust in his arms. "He doesn't care about fancy watches, and those are harder to move than you think. He likes drugs, but those'll just go up his nose in a microsecond. The guy is psycho for music, though. Your big fancy plan about buying him off? It'll actually work if we bring him an icon of West Coast hip-hop."

"I thought he just liked disco."

"Nah, he's a fan of everything. I actually did a job for him once, way back in the day. He was bopping along with Willie Nelson as he tortured a dude with a blowtorch. Even turned it into a karaoke thing, if you can believe it. If the guy could hold the notes, Boz didn't burn him. Didn't last, though."

She shook her head. "God, I should have done literally anything else for a living."

"But you're good at what you do."

"I know. I just can't take the lunatics. Thank you for coming out with me."

"Sure."

"I just hope I'm not leading us into certain doom."

The assassin craned his head around the edge of the arch. The swaying streetlights illuminated nothing but empty pavement for ten blocks in either direction. "A long time ago, I had a contract to assassinate a bad man," he said. "Actually, 'bad man' is something of an understatement. This is the kind of dude who'd sell his own mother into sexual slavery for a buck-fifty and a can of Coke. But like a lot of bad men who make money doing terrible things, he was also intensely paranoid. Lived on the top floor of a luxury high-rise in Billionaire's Row with a ton of security guys around him all day, every day. And he never left. Sound familiar?"

Fiona leaned against the church's wooden doors, her arms wrapped around her chest for a bit more warmth. "Did you get him?"

The assassin chuckled. "You bet I got him. I couldn't go in shooting—they had the stairwell and elevator locked down, and even if I got into the apartment, he had one mother-fucker of a panic room installed. I didn't want to use a bomb, because you set one of those off in Manhattan and every single law-enforcement official in the country gets really interested in nailing your pelt to the wall. Poisoning was out, too."

"Did you talk him to death?"

"You're so funny. No, I managed to get my hands on the building schematics. As it turned out, every apartment in that building was its own little world—thick glass windows, concrete walls, marble floors. This place also had an enormous infinity pool on the roof, as part of this whole complex with a bar and other stuff. Imagine dogpaddling around fifty stories up, right among the skyscrapers—I guess that would make all your bad deeds worth it. Anyway, I snuck up there one night when everyone was gone, dove into the pool, and attached a mining explosive to the bottom."

"I thought you said no bombs."

"I meant 'no bombs' in the sense of fires, shrapnel, shock-wave, all that good stuff. But a mining explosive, like the one I used for this contract, it's meant to crack stone. It drives a lot of force in a very particular direction."

"So, a shaped charge."

"Exactly. I set it up perfectly. The charge blew a big hole in the bottom of the pool, along with the ceiling of the guy's apartment below. All the water flowed through the hole and filled the guy's apartment. Turned it into a fish aquarium. He drowned. The water pressure meant nobody could open the front door, so the cops had to pump the water out through the hole I'd blown."

"And none of it leaked down to the other apartments?"

"Not a drop. Like I said, all those units were sealed absolutely tight. All of which brings me to my point—and yes, I do have a point here. There's nothing that's impossible. We'll get Bill back safe and sound. We'll kill whoever took him. And then we'll go out for pancakes or something, sound good?"

"That was your idea of a motivational speech?"

"Did you like it? I was thinking of taking it on the road. Commencement speeches, state fairs, that kind of thing. Maybe a self-help book in a couple years, once I build an audience. 'Five Lessons on Living Your Best Life from a Master Assassin.'"

"Need to work on that title."

"Well, I need to get some kind of side gig going. I was fired from my job."

"What'd you do, shoot your boss?"

"Nah. Tied him to a chair and tattooed something nasty on his forehead. It's okay, he was a jerk."

Fiona swallowed. "Look, I'm just going to ask this: are you angry about me shooting you?"

The assassin clicked his tongue. "Yeah, but then I got over it. You put me on a different path. Hopefully for the better. In my mind, that makes us even." He nodded down the avenue. "Someone's coming."

Headlights had popped into view maybe seven blocks to the south. She bet it was Boz's RV, right on time despite the apocalypse. You had to hand it to Boz: he was a criminal lunatic, but a punctual one.

An RV was a combat nightmare. Tight space, weird angles. If this went sideways, how would she react? And just like that, bam, she remembered one of the best days of her childhood, when her father—the great and terrible Walker, scourge of the nation's enemies from Managua to Krakow—decided to teach her a little something about clearing a room.

"I know how to clean my room," young Fiona had growled, barely looking up from the Barbie doll she was busy decapitating on the kitchen table.

"No, silly, not cleaning a room," Walker said, offering her the same tight-lipped smile he'd flashed her mother's boyfriend before throwing him off a balcony. "We're going to clear one. Grab a sidearm."

Sounded like fun. Young Fiona opted for her pink watergun, the one with the extra-large reservoir. Walker escorted her into the garage, where he unlocked the massive gun safe beside the tool bench. He chose a 9mm from the racks of pistols and rifles, popped the clip and racked the slide to verify it was unloaded before stuffing it into his belt.

Since the divorce, Walker had moved them onto an enormous parcel of land on the edge of the Barrens. Much of it was overgrown, with thick patches of woodland and scrub virtually impassible with anything short of a machete. It was sometimes hard for Fiona to believe only a quarter of a mile separated their driveway from strip malls, her school, and the great highway plugging into New York City.

Two hundred yards behind the house, on a narrow dirt trail, Walker had built a seven-room building out of plywood. It lacked a roof, but he had installed doors and windows. Each room featured a collection of ratty, moldy furniture scrounged from dumpsters and secondhand stores. Young Fiona knew her father and his friends used this weird structure to practice for work, and she always had to stay in the house whenever they did so. Sitting in her room, she heard the gunfire and sometimes smelled an acrid stench that made her eyes water.

The plywood was pocked with holes from rifles and pistols. They stood before the bright red front door. "There are two types of clearing a room," Walker told her. "Dynamic entry, and the slice."

Standing close to the door, he said, "This is dynamic entry," and kicked above the knob. The door crashed open, and he went in low and fast, moving to the right with his empty pistol in a two-handed grip.

"That's pretty cool," she said.

"You'll get to try it in a moment," Walker said, walking out the door and closing it behind him. "The second, the slice, is safer." He placed his hand on the knob, turned it, and pushed the door open softly. "You see how the door isn't open all the way?"

"Yeah?"

"That blocks off the portion of the room behind the door. Gives you a bit of cover. Sure, someone could shoot through it, but if they're there, hopefully you'll hear them and react before they get a shot off. In the meantime, watch how I move. I'm clearing the room without stepping inside."

Using the same two-handed grip, Walker stood outside the threshold and swiveled slowly from right to left, nodded, and then ducked inside the room, twisting so he covered behind the door. "Got it?" he called.

"Yeah."

Walker slammed the door shut, then yelled through it:

"Count to ten, then execute a dynamic entry. I'll be in here somewhere."

They spent the afternoon practicing how to assault a house. After a brief break, they went "full ammo," which meant Fiona filled her water gun at the backyard tap and tried to spray her father upon entry, even tagging him once or twice. By the time the reddening sun touched the far trees, she had become quite good at dynamic entry, although she was still too impatient to master the slice.

It was one of the best days of her life.

It would be another fifteen years before she did it for real, of course, but she always liked to think her survival to this point was due to her dear father hammering these lessons home so early.

Decades later, as rain slashed Park Avenue to ribbons, Fiona stared at the flank of Boz's approaching hurricane-proof RV and almost barked laughter. She'd crossed a lot of thresholds and smashed her way into a lot of rooms—but this was a new one. On the RV's flank, three slim stairs rose to a windowless metal door.

If Boz wanted to kill them, anyone inside the vehicle had every advantage: height, plus the narrow door restricting an outsider's ability to see anything other than a bit of the interior. Boz had covered the windows with sheet metal, rendering the inside invisible from every angle except the windshield and front passenger windows, which were tinted.

As the RV rumbled to the curb, splashing a wave of water before it, the door cracked open. An enormous head in a bright yellow slicker poked out. "Come on," the head growled.

The assassin bowed at the waist, beckoning for her to lead off.

"Such a gentleman," Fiona said, and darted from the stone

archway to the RV's door, the rain like a fire hose to the face. She scrambled up the ladder, the assassin on her heels. She had her hand inside her raincoat, finger on the trigger of the pistol, trying to blink the water from her eyes as fast as she could.

When her vision returned, her first impression was that the RV reminded her of a dive bar. A web of multicolored lights dangled from the narrow ceiling, bathing the interior in slickly shades of purple and yellow. To the left, the rear sleeping nook was a thicket of electronics: PC towers and servers and half-dismantled equipment with wires and bits dangling out, everything linked in odd ways, lights blinking, drives humming. To the right, a leopard-print bench stretched beneath a line of three deer skulls painted blue, white, and red. Beside the bench hummed a small fridge loaded with baggies of weed, rows of beers and energy drinks.

Boz sat at the small table across the aisle from the couch, dressed in a tank top four sizes too small. The tank top featured an illustration of a pink unicorn shitting a rainbow. He also wore pants, thankfully, although Fiona knew that was never a certain thing with him. He had an enormous laptop open before him, its white glow playing over his huge head, his lanky hair draped over his shoulders.

Beside Boz stood two men, so enormous they had to crouch so their heads wouldn't scrape the ceiling. One wore a yellow slicker, and the other was dressed in what Fiona liked to call Standard Bouncer Style: black t-shirt to show off the basketball-sized biceps, black pants, black sneakers. Tonight was all about the oversized bodyguards. Just once, why couldn't she end up in a dangerous situation with people close to her own size?

The assassin filed in behind her, shutting the door behind

him. He regarded the two men, his eyebrow cocked. "Let me guess," he said. "You guys weigh what, two-forty, two-fifty each?"

"Two-thirty," said the guy in the yellow slicker.

"Two-thirty-five," the guy behind him offered.

The assassin snorted. "I bet you need to eat, like, four thousand calories of protein per day, right, maintain that muscle mass?"

"Who are you?" Boz snapped at him.

A steel wall blocked the driver's area from the rest of the RV. It lacked a door, but had a small window at chest height, blocked by a sliding cover. The metal was painted with a mural of a laughing green skull.

"I'm nobody," the assassin said. "Who are you?"

"He's with me," Fiona said. "That's all you need to know."

"You both vaccinated?" Boz asked.

"Yeah," Fiona said.

"I get a booster shot every day, just for the thrill of it," the assassin said.

"What's that in your hands?" Boz pointed at the Tupac bust.

"A gift," the assassin said, turning the bust so they had a better view of the face. "You like?"

"Oh, I like," Boz smiled. "Get a little California love up in here, you know what I'm saying? Come on in."

"Wait." The bodyguard in the raincoat raised a hand. "We got to search you."

"God, not again," Fiona said.

The bodyguard snorted. "Excuse me?"

"We're armed, if that makes any difference. But we're not going to be the first ones to do anything stupid," Fiona said, unslinging her waterproof backpack and tossing it beside Boz's feet. "There's another little gift for you."

The roof was insulated, reducing the rain to a drumming faint enough for Fiona to hear the bodyguards breathing heavily, ready for violence. Wind rocked the RV, and she braced a hand against the nearest wall.

"Relax," Boz told his muscle. "I know 'em."

The raincoated bodyguard's face twitched. The other guard stepped to his right for a clearer view.

Boz unzipped the backpack and jammed a hand inside, swirling around a couple hundred thousand dollars' worth of fine timepieces. "This is okay, I guess."

"Yeah, you guess," Fiona said. "It's worth about a quarter-million, we figure. We cool?"

"I like the big gold head better. You want to bring that up here?" Boz zipped the backpack closed and tossed it behind him.

The assassin handed the bust to one of the guards, who tried to act as if it weighed nothing as he turned and hoisted it onto a small shelf to the right of the deer skulls.

"But I can't do anything about that guy whose penthouse you hit. He really wants that girl back," Boz said.

"Who is he?" Fiona sighed. "And don't you dare tell me it doesn't matter, that I can't do anything about it. It's my life at risk."

"It's Kurt Beau," Boz said.

"Never heard of him," the assassin said.

Boz squinted at him. "No reason you should have. You know there's a list of billionaires, right? The world's richest?"

"Sure?" Fiona said.

"He's high up there, but he's not one of those flashy ones who you see giving money to charity, setting up foundations, whatever. In fact, it's hard to tell how exactly he made all that filthy treasure." Boz flashed yellow teeth. "All great fortunes are built on a pile of bodies, you know?"

The assassin asked, "What if we give the girl back?"

Boz shook his head. "Won't help. You raided one of his houses. He wants blood."

Fiona snorted. "It's your fault, dude. It would have been a clean raid, except you had no idea where the fucking server was. I should never have taken the gig."

Boz shrugged. "But you did. You wanted what I have to offer. A new identity? Healthcare? A fake name in a bunch of databases? Come on, Fiona, going legit is so boring. Would have been so easy to give it to you, too, except you had to go and rescue someone you had no right rescuing. But you gave me a cool gold head of Tupac. Now get off my party-mobile."

"No," Fiona said.

The bodyguards shifted.

Boz shut his laptop and giggled. "Excuse me?"

"I told you before: we need a ride," she said. "To the West Side and up. There's a warehouse there."

"Can't it wait until after the storm?" Boz asked, waving his hand at the roof.

Fiona shook her head. "It's life or death."

"Everything in the middle of a hurricane is life or death." Boz leaned back, his belly rising beneath the tank top like unbaked dough. "Fine. We're headed north anyway. You're lucky you caught us so close to you."

"Thank you," Fiona said, meaning it.

"I'd ask to sit down," the assassin said. "But I'm afraid if I did that, I'd catch a juicy case of hepatitis or something."

"Who is this guy?" one of the guards muttered.

"Someone who doesn't want to be hooked up to an IV of antibiotics for the rest of his life," the assassin said. "I don't mean any offense, of course. Thank you for driving us. I just have no filter."

"Me neither," Boz said, rapping his knuckles three times against the bulkhead.

The engine roared and the RV lurched forward, powering up Park Avenue. Fiona leaned against the wall opposite the assassin. Her mouth sour with fear, her nerves sizzling. She had a belly full of protein, at least, but how much longer could she go before she dropped from outright exhaustion?

Just save Bill.

Right. Wouldn't be the first time. She loved her husband with all her heart, but he was a real pain in the ass.

"How much do you think Beau would pay for you?" Boz said, leaning back and lacing his hands behind his head, as if it was a casual question asked over a cool beer or two.

"I don't care," Fiona said, placing her hand on her jacket, her thumb skimming the contours of her gun. In her peripheral vision, the assassin locked eyes with the two bodyguards, who stared at them with the barely restrained hunger of big cats.

18

THE COP CRUISER rumbled into the depot, bringing a blast of rain that wet the concrete almost to Bill's feet. The door rolled back down, rattling against the wind. Before it closed, Bill saw the street outside flooded with a foot or two of murky water. A low white building across the street.

"Oh shit," Crew Cut said.

The cruiser's doors opened, and two uniformed cops stepped out, pulling down the black nylon balaclavas from their lower faces to reveal a pair of kids, no more than twenty-one or twenty-two. Their gazes thrumming with tension.

"Who are you?" Crew Cut asked, walking toward them.

"Officer Lawrence," said the cruiser's driver, a blonde kid with a square head.

"Officer Pembry," offered the other one, darker, with a slimmer build than his partner. "Identify yourselves."

Crew Cut shot Bill a warning glance before swiveling back

to the cops. "I'm reaching into my belt for my badge. I'm Lieutenant Michael King, 19th Precinct."

"Go ahead," Officer Lawrence said, a little shaky, his hands loose at his side instead of hovering above his pistol or stun gun.

Crew Cut drew a leather billfold from his pocket and let it fall open, revealing the badge. "We were taking this suspect into custody," he nodded toward Bill, "but the storm made it too dangerous to move, so we took refuge here."

Office Pembry glanced at the others around the table. "You're also cops?"

Katzen and Hardaway introduced themselves, flashing their badges. Tatoo and Soul Patch did the same, naming themselves: Sergeant Brooks and Sergeant Bowler of the 17th Precinct, respectively.

"Yeah, it's bad out there," Officer Lawrence said. "We were supposed to help out with the roadblock they're setting up on Riverside Boulevard, because the water's coming up, but..."

Officer Pembry pointed at the front of the police cruiser, its headlights shattered and its fender cracked.

"No way it's flooding," Crew Cut said. "No way. It's like a hundred feet down to the water there."

"I know." Officer Lawrence nodded. "The roadblock's so people don't drive down. The power, it's going out all along the West Side. Maybe further south, too."

"We still got it here," Katzen said.

"Like that means anything," Crew Cut snapped. "Who knows how long the whole fucking grid will hold."

"You guys got any coffee or anything?" Officer Pembry asked. "We're cold as shit."

"Sure," Hardaway said, gesturing toward the coffee machine on the far table. "I'll make you some."

"Thanks," Officer Pembry said, glancing at Bill. "Your perp. What's his story?"

"Excessive rock 'n rolling," Bill said.

"Ignore him," Hardaway said. "It's a fraud case."

A low purr as the coffee machine ground up pods and spewed hot coffee into paper cups. Hardaway carried the cups to the officers, who drifted to the long table without so much as a second glance at Bill.

Tattoo exchanged a look with Crew Cut, who shook his head. Katzen shoved Bill's notes on North Brother Island into the leather folder.

"Good coffee," Officer Pembry said, taking a sip.

"Don't need to butter me up," Hardaway said. "It's called Rain Forest Melody, or something, but it tastes like shit. It's okay, you can admit it."

"I've had better," Officer Lawrence offered, his gaze drifting over the walls and floor before settling on Bill's shattered smartwatch. A quick blink, and his eyes moved along. No change in his expression.

"Where you out of?" Soul Patch asked.

"Ninth," Officer Pembry said.

"You're a long way from home," Katzen offered.

"Everybody's out there," Officer Lawrence said. "Just trying to hold this shit together."

The lights blinked out.

Someone gasped. A chair rasped on the concrete.

The dull rumble of thunder like artillery.

Bill stood. Should he run? Try to sneak away? It was too quiet in here—they'd hear him. If he moved to the table, they might mistake him for one of them. You could grab a gun, he told himself. Then you have a chance. No, no chance. You'll die.

So what? You're dying anyway!

True. He stepped toward the table, holding his breath so he could hear better. A metallic click, either a chair settling or a thumb on a holster. A low curse.

"Get a flashlight," Crew Cut called out.

The lights flickered on.

Bill was already back in his seat, cursing himself. *Maybe if you'd been a little faster, you could have done something. Saved your own ass, instead of waiting for your wife to save you. Again.*

"It'll happen again," Hardaway said. "This place has a backup generator?"

Crew Cut snorted. "Not that I'm aware of."

"Listen, I have a suggestion," Officer Pembry said. "You have that armored carrier over there. We could pack everyone in it, head to the nearest station."

Officer Lawrence's shoulder radio crackled: "...ort in..."

Slugging down the rest of his coffee, Officer Lawrence stepped away from the table, muttering into the handset. He stopped between his cruiser and the rattling roll-up doors.

Crew Cut stretched and bent to touch his toes—one, two, three, four. Stunningly supple for an older dude. Beyond him, Soul Patch and Tattoo circled toward the coffee machine. They were creating space, Bill realized. Ready for something bad to happen.

Katzen was paler than before. Hardaway coughed and rubbed her face. They were nervous and trying to hide it. Bill strained to catch anything from the conversation between Officer Lawrence and whoever was on the other side of that radio, but the rumble of the storm made it impossible to pick out anything but a few words: "...warehouse...personnel..."

If someone starts shooting, Bill thought, you better tip

your chair over. Crawl for a door. If you're lucky, you won't catch a stray. If you're extra-lucky, everyone will be too busy killing each other to focus on you.

On the table, another radio crackled: "King, you there?"

Crew Cut froze.

"King," the radio crackled again. "Report in."

"Give me the radio," Crew Cut told Hardaway, who was closer.

Hardaway tossed him the radio, which Crew Cut caught one-handed.

"Yeah, I'm here," Crew Cut told the radio.

Hardaway pretended to scratch her back, drawing up the back of her jacket, revealing the grip of her pistol.

"You better give me a sit-rep," the radio crackled. "They're saying you left your post, you dumb asshole."

"Yeah, I responded to an all-hands arrest," Crew Cut said, his eyes locked on the two young officers. "We arrested the suspect, but we've taken refuge in one of the vehicle depots. We'll get back when we can."

"What…" the radio dissolved into static.

"Bad copy," Crew Cut said. "Please repeat."

"Wh—pect?" Crackle, crackle. "What arrest? Nobody—"

Officer Pembry backed away from the table. He didn't have his hand on his gun—not yet—but he could sense something wasn't right. Beside the garage door, Officer Lawrence heard something in his radio that made him jolt upright.

Another radio on the table crackled. "Hardaway, come in," a voice snapped.

Officer Pembry's hand drifted toward his waist.

The radio again: "Hardaway, where the hell are you?"

Bill tensed his legs, ready to dive.

"What's going on?" Officer Pembry asked, low and casual.

Hardaway's hands behind her back, yanking her weapon from her waistband, but Officer Pembry must have been the fastest gun at the Policy Academy because he had already dropped his coffee and drawn his weapon in a two-handed grip, no way could he miss from this distance.

Hardaway, Crew Cut, Tattoo and Soul Patch also drew their guns.

Shouting from the direction of the garage doors. Officer Lawrence crouched behind the rear bumper of his cruiser, only his gun and part of his face visible. Ordering everyone to drop their weapons.

Nobody listened to him.

Bill tried to judge potential angles of fire. No guns were pointed in his direction, but bullets had a way of ricocheting off concrete and metal. If he stayed in this chair, he was a fat target. If he threw himself to the floor, he might startle someone into firing at him.

"Everybody, let's calm the fuck down," Crew Cut snapped.

Officer Pembry lowered his pistol so it pointed at Hardaway's chest instead of her head. As he did so, Tattoo and Soul Patch dipped their barrels to the floor.

But Katzen kept his firearm locked on Officer Pembry's head. Maybe he was triggered by someone pointing a gun at his partner. "Drop that gun," he told the younger cop. "You drop it right now."

"You tell me what's going on," Officer Pembry said.

"It's some corrupt shit," Officer Lawrence offered from his cover behind the pillar. "Radio told me. They're hunting for them."

Crew Cut spun on Katzen. "I thought you had everything covered."

Katzen snorted. "That dumb fuck in IA. He was onto me from the beginning. I knew it."

"You asshole," Tattoo said. "I knew we couldn't trust this fucker."

"It's all fixable," Hardaway said. She stared at Officer Pembry like a cobra hypnotizing its prey, unblinking. "Nobody needs to get hurt here."

"We were blown anyway," Katzen said, taking three steps to his left so he could focus on Crew Cut and Officer Pembry at the same time. "We all got debts. Alimony. Gambling, in my case. Mortgages. And you think the city's giving us what we need? What we deserve? We're owed this. These two fine officers here, I'm sorry, but they're just going to have to go."

"The fuck," Officer Lawrence shouted. "You fire, you die first, you understand? You die first."

Crew Cut tapped his gun against his leg. "Nobody has to die tonight. But officers, I'm going to have to ask you to toss those weapons. We're going to handcuff you, place you in your cruiser. That will provide us more than enough time to get out of here."

Officer Lawrence glanced at Bill.

"Don't look at me," Bill said. "I'm just the hostage here."

"Cover me, partner," Officer Pembry said. "I'm coming back."

"Move," Officer Lawrence said.

Pembry backed up, trusting his partner to cover him. If these young dudes have a shotgun in their cruiser, Bill thought, it could change the odds yet again.

Katzen shook his head.

Pembry was almost to the cruiser. Almost near cover.

"No," Katzen said, his finger tensing on the trigger. "We got to do it."

Crew Cut raised his pistol and fired.

Blood spat from Katzen's skull. He toppled to the floor, his weapon skittering away.

Hardaway dropped her pistol and raised her hands, her fingers trembling. "I can live with it," she told Crew Cut.

An engine roared. The door of the cruiser open, Officer Pembry scrambling onto the front passenger seat. Officer Lawrence running low across the concrete floor, barely slowing as he dove over Pembry and into the driver's seat. Under other circumstances, the flailing acrobatics would have been funny.

The cruiser reversed, smashing into the roll-up door hard enough to tear the lower half away. Its undercarriage sparked as it bounced down the driveway and into the street, its rear bumper plowing an enormous wave of dirty water. A fast slide, the squeal of brakes, and it powered south, engine screaming over the storm's howl.

"I'm glad we didn't kill them," Tattoo said.

"I am, too," Crew Cut said. "You remember what it was like, being that young? Damn, you thought you were actually doing some good. Let's get everyone in the APC. We're going to that fucking island right now."

19

EVERY TIME THE RV swayed in the punishing wind, Fiona's stomach flipped. Every time the huge tires plowed through another pothole, she braced herself against the nearest wall. The driver was a big-rig cowboy, pushing the gas far too hard for conditions. She could only hope he avoided running over anything living.

The bodyguards sat on the couch, their hands on their knees, vibrating with ill intent.

In his command chair, Boz clicked a laptop key every few seconds, pretending to ignore them.

Fiona scanned the space for weapons. Boz probably had a shotgun wired to the underside of his table, hidden by the short tablecloth. The bodyguards had enough muscles to twist off her head like a bottlecap, and she bet they also had pistols tucked down the backs of their pants.

"Relax," Boz finally said. "You paid me enough for this little trip."

"And after?" Fiona asked.

Boz shrugged. "We're still good, provided we don't cross paths ever again, dig?"

"I dig."

Boz shifted to the assassin. "You giving me the shit-eye, friend?"

The assassin shrugged. "Nope."

"Good." Boz nodded. "Real good. Because there's something you should know about me: I'm such a badass, I'm guilty of crimes they haven't even invented yet."

The assassin brightened. "Like fucking a space alien?"

Boz squinted in confusion. "What?"

"Kidnapping a tiger and driving it across state lines?" The assassin grinned, enjoying this.

Boz shook his head. "Look, forget it. The point is, we're all sitting here, having as good a time as we can in the middle of a major storm, and I don't need you eyeing me, okay—"

A rapping on the bulkhead. Boz rapped back before sliding open the cover, revealing the driver's ice-blue eyes. "Getting close," the driver said. "No way anyone's getting out in this shit, though."

"Thanks." Boz slammed the cover shut and tapped a few more keys on the laptop. "The eye's almost overhead, according to this. Another forty minutes, maybe? Then it'll be clear."

"That'll be a relief," Fiona said.

"Truly." Boz clicked another window, and his brow scrunched in concentration. He snapped his fingers, and the bodyguards' heads swiveled in his direction. Boz tilted the laptop so they had a better view.

One of the bodyguards whistled. The other one gave

Fiona an appraising look she didn't like at all. She slipped her hand beneath her jacket, her thumb on the pistol's cold steel. Beside her, the assassin tensed.

Boz's hands stayed on the laptop's keyboard. If they slipped beneath the table, she would have to do something.

"What's up?" she asked through a clenched jaw.

"Nothing," Boz said. "Just something funny online."

"Why don't you tell us?" the assassin rasped. He was no longer the jokester in the polyester Elvis costume, no. This was the boogeyman who stalked the nighttime streets of too many cities, just as ready to kill you with either a paintbrush or a sniper rifle.

Boz's left hand drifted beneath the table.

Boz started to say, "It has to do with…"

Fiona yanked at her pistol but it snagged on the lining of her wet jacket, and she was already too late, Boz was about to—

The world imploded.

The RV wall dented inward, as if slammed by a giant boot.

Bodyguards flew across the space, a quarter-ton of gym-toned beef crashing into Boz.

The RV tilted, the wall becoming the floor as Fiona slid across it, the assassin tumbling beside her. A hard rain of bottles and glasses and bullets and hard drives, sex toys like deep-sea creatures in glowing pink and blue, pills in all colors of the rainbow, and a leopard-print bra.

With a bone-rattling boom, the RV landed on its side. Fiona took a deep breath and patted her body for anything broken. Nope, all good. Beside her, the assassin poked his head up and groaned.

Below her, water gurgled through a tear in the RV's door. Oily water, deepening quickly.

There were no windows in here. If the water filled the

RV—and there was more than enough water outside to do that—they would drown in the middle of the street, inches from the open air.

She started laughing.

"What's so funny?" the assassin slurred.

"Two car crashes in one night. What are the odds?" She rolled and rose onto her knees, hoping everyone else in the RV was dead.

The bodyguards were dead or unconscious, their bulk pinning Boz's legs. Boz's upper half twisted against the wall, his tank top torn away to reveal pasty flesh, his cracked laptop still in his grip. The cracked screen displayed a browser-based version of the same app the assassin had shown her in the subway.

It was the bidding page for her death.

Even if her idea of the Bitcoin exchange rate was way off, the bidding was now up to a cool million dollars.

Wonderful.

Boz's head stirred, and his bloodshot eyes opened. "Don't," he said.

"Don't what?" Fiona asked, standing.

"Don't take my red wagon," Boz said, frowning.

Diagnosis: concussion. "No worries on that, buddy," Fiona said. The crash had stripped the cushions from the bench, revealing a storage space with an arsenal of weapons and ammunition strapped to the bottom. She selected an MP5 submachine gun finished in bright pink, a popular cartoon cat etched into the grip.

"It's very you," the assassin said. "Hand me that pump-action shotgun beside it, will ya? Box of ammo would be nice, too."

She did, and he upended the box of 12-gauge shells into his pocket. "Let's see what we hit, huh?" he said.

The water was two inches deep, pooling around her ankles, and rising fast. They needed an out. Now.

A drop of water smacked her forehead. She looked up at the wall-turned-ceiling. Water pooled around a crack in the fake wood paneling. Balancing on the edge of the overturned table, she gripped the edge of the paneling and yanked as hard as her tired muscles allowed.

The paneling cracked. So did something in her shoulder. Pain blazed down her back.

"You okay?" the assassin asked.

"Yeah."

"Plenty of pills floating down here, if you're not."

"Nope, I'm good." She gripped the jagged edge of the panel, took a deep breath, and pulled again. A larger piece snapped away. She winced.

"Like, this purple one," the assassin continued. "It's either a painkiller or you'll see neon elephants."

"Stop." Rain poured through the new gap, cool on her face. Shredded metal beyond. A hole right to the outside, the air whistling around. Reversing the MP5 in her grip, she slammed the stock against the ragged edges, soggy bits of paneling slapping her cheeks, water in her eyes. The whistling air deepened into a roar, a fiercer wind scattering pills and bullets and scraps of paper.

Now she had widened the hole enough to wriggle through. Slinging the ridiculous pink gun around her shoulder, she gripped the edges and hoisted herself onto the outside of the RV—rain and wind slapping her blind. She almost slid headfirst off the edge.

Placing a hand over her eyes, she squinted at the street

below. An NYPD cruiser, of all damn things, had crashed into the RV. Its lights were off, its hood accordioned into crumpled metal. The storm made it impossible to see a driver behind the wheel, or any passengers.

"Hey, should I grab the Tupac head?" the assassin called. "It's right up in the corner here. Like, *embedded* in the wall. Although I guess it's the ceiling now."

"Come out right now or I'm leaving you." She stuck her hand through the hole. The assassin gripped it as he emerged, wincing as his gut snagged on the hole's rough edges.

"Like toothpaste in a tube," he said, offering her a sorry little grin, and she felt a flush of pity and sadness for this man she once shot in the back.

"Watch out once you're up, it's slippery," she said. It was windy, too, but the RV lay at an angle that blocked at least some of it.

"Oh, I got it," he said, full of bravado—and almost slid right off. Once he firmed his grip, Fiona poked her head back into the RV. The rising water maybe a foot deep now, the bodyguards face-down in it, unmoving. Dead.

Boz was alive, though. His lips peeled back to reveal bloody teeth. A sawed-off shotgun in his shaking grip.

"Red wagon," Boz said, raising the weapon. Fiona ducked back, already knowing it was hopeless—at this range, the pellets would punch through the RV's skin, tagging her anyway. Her movement rocked the RV no more than an inch, but it was enough to set a miracle in motion.

The gold bust of Tupac, lodged in the corner of the wall-turned-ceiling, tumbled loose. It fell straight down, heavier than a bowling ball, and the Rap God's forehead hit Boz's nose with a meaty thump.

Fiona winced. As much as she hated Boz, she hoped the

man was dead after a hit like that. She rolled away from the hole, offering the assassin a hearty thumbs-up.

The RV had crunched to its final resting place on one of the wider north-south avenues running up the West Side. They were a few blocks north of Hudson Yards, the city's ultra-luxury development. The lights dimmed, flared, dimmed again. A bad sign. If the power died for the city's richest and most famous, everyone else was screwed, too.

"Let's take the cruiser," the assassin said, and slid down the flank of the RV to the street, which was flooded to mid-shin, slick with oil and filled with paper and cans and other debris. Fiona dropped beside him, unslinging the submachine gun as she circled around the passenger side of the police cruiser.

The windows were smashed into milky cataracts. She opened the door, revealing two cops slumped in their seats, the baggy mess of an airbag sagging from the steering wheel. She jabbed two fingers into the cool skin of the nearest cop's neck. Strong pulse.

"Wha?" the cop murmured, awakened by the harsh touch. His nameplate said 'PEMBRY.'

"Are you okay?" Fiona reached across him to check the pulse of the other cop, whose nameplate said 'LAWRENCE.' Another strong heartbeat. Ah, these young guys, full of muscle and vigor.

Officer Lawrence's eyes fluttered open. "Fu…"

"Stay there," Fiona said, pulling the cops' service weapons from their holsters. Unloaded and pocketed the clips, kicked the empty weapons into the flood.

"RV driver's dead," the assassin said, reappearing at her side. The door shielded them from the wind, but Fiona needed to brace her spine against the handle to keep it open.

Officer Pembry's eyes opened, unfocused, drifting from Fiona to the assassin to the cracked dashboard. "Who're you?"

"Doesn't matter," Fiona said. "Are you okay?"

Officer Pembry's shaking hand fumbled for the radio clipped to his shoulder. Hitting the button, he slurred, "Depot... hostage..."

"I don't think that's working, buddy," the assassin said.

"What hostage?" Fiona asked. "Was it a guy in a suit? Dark hair, kind of suave?"

"'Kind of suave'?" The assassin snorted. "That's no way to describe someone. What next? 'He smelled like regret and too much vodka'?"

"Shut up," she said, turning back to Officer Pembry. "What hostage?"

Officer Pembry nodded slowly. "Man in a suit. Dark hair. Kept... making... jokes."

"Look," the assassin said, pointing toward the cruiser's rear. It was difficult to see more than a block through the overpowering rain, but the glow from the surrounding buildings illuminated what looked like a black tank without a turret crossing the intersection. Fiona thought it looked like an APC, one of those armored personnel carriers that patrolled the streets of Baghdad and Kabul before the Defense Department donated them to police forces across the country. Because nothing says community policing like a vehicle designed for heavy assaults.

If Bill was in there, they were getting away.

"Gotta call it in," Officer Pembry burbled, hands slapping his seatbelt. He was groggy, but for how much longer? "Gotta—"

"Easy, buddy," Fiona said.

Officer Lawrence stirred again, rubbing his head, and asked, "What'd we hit?"

"An RV," Fiona said, and when the cop turned toward her, offered him a dead-eyed stare. "Some people were hurt on that RV."

Officer Lawrence was in better shape than his colleague, his eyes clearer. His attention locked on her gun. "Okay," he said, nodding.

"You better check on them. You and your partner."

"Okay," Officer Lawrence said, nodding, as his door opened and the assassin reached in to grip his shoulder, levering him out of the vehicle and into the rain. The cop yelped, either in protest or because of the cold water.

As Fiona dragged out the cop closer to her, something flashed overhead—a twisted piece of metal, maybe a sign, warbling in the wind. Another few feet lower, and it might have sliced through them like a buzzsaw.

Fiona left the assassin to escort the two cops into the relative shelter of the RV as she slid into the driver's seat, annoyed at how her feet barely touched the pedals. She tried adjusting the seat, but it refused to move. The impact must have broken the mechanism.

"Do you need a box?" the assassin asked, sliding into the passenger seat.

"Shut the fuck up," Fiona said. Throwing the car into reverse, she stood on the gas, concerned about the engine's rattling roar but downright worried about the cracked, leaking windows. Zero visibility out there. At least they were looking for a tank—hard to miss one of those on empty streets, right?

"You know where they're going, right?" the assassin asked.

At the intersection, Fiona braked, shifted, and steered the car east. "North Brother Island, if we don't catch them in time."

And then every light in Manhattan flickered out.

20

FIVE MINUTES INTO their bumping APC ride across the city, Bill started praying none of these cops had decided to down a heavy protein load within the past five hours. A fart or belch would linger in the tiny space forever, trapped by layers of steel and whatever other taxpayer-funded space-age polymers the Pentagon inserted into these vehicles.

Bill thought about cracking a joke to that effect—"Please, nobody toot."—but the mood in the tight space was too grim. Sitting on the steel bench beside Soul Patch, Crew Cut seemed ready to pistol-whip anyone who opened their mouth. Next to Bill, Hardaway stared at her hands. Tattoo drove, a silhouette in the driver's seat.

"You get your partner's share," Crew Cut told Hardaway, loud over the rain hammering the APC's roof. "And don't give me any kind of weepy shit. I know you hated him as much as we did."

Hardaway shrugged. "What's done is done."

"That's a girl," Soul Patch offered. "Chances are good those goody two-shoes fucks are calling anyone they can raise on the radio."

These cops are finished, Bill thought. Over. Everything they had, everything they spent their lives working for—vaporized as if it never existed. Sure, they might find this money on North Brother, but how far will it get them? A couple of years on the run? He had spent years on the run. It wasn't any way to live.

Crew Cut turned to stare at Bill, as if trying to read his thoughts, and Bill looked away, toward Tattoo and the front of the vehicle. The view outside the windshield was nonexistent, a blur of water reflected by the headlights, but at least the vehicle's weight made it impervious to the wind. They could roll over a sedan and barely feel it.

"I'm sorry about your partner," Bill told Hardaway.

"Shut your mouth," she snapped.

"No, I really am. He was a nice guy." Bill used his most confidential tone: "He didn't deserve to go out like that."

"He made his choice." She didn't sound convinced.

I can't flip her, Bill thought. There's just not enough time to build a rapport, not with these guys standing right there. But if she stays angry at everyone, maybe it'll slow down her reaction times when—

"It's not going to work," Hardaway said.

Bill startled. "Huh?"

"Whatever you're planning." She leaned back against the rumbling metal. "Just get us to the money, okay? Then we'll let you go."

Bill turned to Crew Cut. "You got a boat ready?"

Crew Cut nodded. "Made that call before we left."

"Okay." Bill said. "You know how I was on the run for a long time? Yeah, you do. You saw the file. I know how to get you fake IDs, everything you need to build a new life once you've got the money."

"Shut up," Soul Patch said.

"No, let him speak," Crew Cut said.

"I know you don't trust me," Bill continued, warming to his theme. "But you know I have the right contacts. You've spent a lot of time on the street, you know what's legit and what's not. I'm not saying you couldn't do it yourself, but I can help you get set up faster. And after this, you'll need all the speed you can get."

"We'll think about it," Crew Cut said, and Bill could sense his interest like an electric charge. It was exciting to worm your way into someone's head, play with their emotions and their view of the world. Maybe I shouldn't give up the con quite yet, Bill thought. Maybe this kind of thing is what I'm meant to do.

Just as long as you don't get killed.

True, but that was always the problem, wasn't it? If he survived this, and if he stayed true to the hustle, he'd need to figure out a way of life that involved less risk of violent death. Like internet fraud.

Up front, Tattoo grunted and twisted the wheel to the left. Bill tumbled across the narrow aisle, almost plowing into Hardaway. Above the constant rumble of rain on metal came another sound, a bone-shaking crackle that reminded Bill of rocks tumbling down a slope—

Through the windshield, a flicker of red and white, followed by a titanic wave of mud—

"Like back in Fallujah!" Tattoo yelped, spinning the wheel in the opposite direction. The APC jolted, rising until it pointed at the howling abyss of the sky. Through the tiny port above his head, Bill glimpsed gray boxes of some sort, a darting blur, maybe a panicked human—

"Whole damn building façade came down," Soul Patch said, sounding almost awed.

The APC crested, dipped, and rumbled down the far side of a sudden hill. Bill's stomach flipped. He guessed they had just climbed over a pile of fresh rubble. He hoped nobody was buried under it. The vehicle crashed onto the street hard enough to slam his tailbone into the bench.

"The eye is here soon," Crew Cut muttered under his breath, his head darting like a bird as he tried to find a better view out of any of the windows. "It's here soon, it's here soon."

Had the rain slackened a little? Impossible to tell. As the APC rumbled along, its headlights the only glow for at least several blocks around, Bill realized he'd rarely felt lonelier and more isolated than right now, surrounded by ten million people. He just hoped Fiona had figured out how to follow him. Baby, I'm not sure I can survive this on my own.

21

THE DRIVE WAS a nightmare. The cruiser's engine performed better than Fiona had any right to expect, given the colossal amount of water pouring through the crumpled hood. It bucked and whined like a dying horse but still rolled them along at five miles an hour. Between the Manhattan blackout and the shattered windshield, the world was reduced to impenetrable murk. She had to steer by feel, jerking the wheel toward the middle of the street whenever her front bumper tapped the flank of a parked car.

"The APC," Fiona said. "The depot the officer mentioned. Why would cops kidnap Bill?"

"Who knows?" the assassin shrugged, visibly irritated by the water spattering through a crimp in his door. "Makes as much sense as anything else."

"I love my husband," she said. "But he's the world's biggest shit magnet."

The assassin snorted. "You two, you could have gone anywhere, right? Why stay here, in New York? Why not Capri?"

She shook her head. "We were planning on leaving. After we got new identities. Not just fake passports—the full package, work history, healthcare, pensions, everything."

"Why? So you could play suburban housewife somewhere?"

She bashed the cruiser into the flank of yet another parked car, the fender crunching hard enough for her to feel through the steering wheel. Damn. She eased back into the middle of the street again, hoping the fender wasn't loose. If it sawed a tire, they were done. How far ahead was the APC? Two avenues? Three?

"Sorry," the assassin said, mistaking her silence for irritation. "That was cruel."

"Not a suburban life," she said. "Just the opportunity to start fresh. Really fresh."

They reached the edge of Times Square. Not that she could see anything with all those garish billboards flicked off. The wind roared through empty space, rocking the cruiser on its springs, and—

Whack!

Something heavy bounced off the roof and spun away.

The assassin yelped.

Fiona pushed the gas, trying to use the power of positive thinking for once in her miserable life. Envisioning a street totally clear all the way to the East River except for a foot or two of water, no car wrecks or stalled ambulances or kids deciding to stunt a TikTok dance video in the middle of a disaster. Envisioning the APC with Bill no more than a block or two ahead of them, slowed by the storm. And if she could just catch up—

"Speaking as someone who knows a little bit about vicious ambushes," the assassin said, "why don't we head to North Brother? Intercept them?"

He was right. She knew it. The APC was too far ahead, with no way of powering this busted-up cruiser fast enough to catch a tank built for literally the worst conditions on Earth. For all she knew, Bill's captors weren't headed due east anymore. "It's not the worst idea," she said. "Except for the lack of a boat."

"Didn't Bill have a plan for a boat?"

"Yeah, one of his yahoo friends."

"Call them."

"What?"

"Do it. Promise them whatever it takes. If they're a yahoo, they got a death wish. Trust me on that one. They'll do it."

Fiona's fingers drummed the steering wheel. "Fine," she said, pulling out her phone and flicking it on. Her face tense in the screen's eldritch light. "Look at that, got signal."

"It was meant to be."

She dialed, put the phone on speaker, and slotted it into the dashboard. Two rings, a click, a burst of static resolving into a confused voice. Fiona launched into it, honey one moment and terrifying the next, playing Bill's contact like a violin.

As they crept along, the rain slackened from Hurricane Force to something approaching Normal Thunderstorm. The eye was almost here, bringing a few hours of calmer weather with it.

The call ended. The assassin shook his head and whistled. "They rode it out in the Newtown Creek?"

"Guess they didn't want to leave the boat," Fiona said,

checking her watch. The guy on the phone had said twenty minutes. They had enough time.

"Surprised the boat isn't kindling."

"Good thing for us."

Fifteen minutes later, they crested the downslope to the East River. The FDR was under two feet of water, threatening to float the cruiser as she pushed down the gas. They rumbled beneath the overpass and stopped before a line of concrete barriers separating the road from the piers and ferry crossings studding the Manhattan coastline.

"That them?" the assassin asked, pointing beyond the CitiBike dock at the edge of the overpass's overhang. The rain slowed to a drizzle, the bruised clouds swirling above. Their cracked windshield framed two human silhouettes at the edge of the ferry landing.

"Yeah," she said, unlocking her seatbelt.

"Tell me more about these guys."

"Old friend of Bill's. Runs guns. He's odd, but what else is new? Not sure how well Bill knows the ship captain, but he's lunatic enough to give us a ride in this."

She put her shoulder to her door, opening it. There was six inches of water on the roadway but none on the pier side of the concrete barriers. Maybe the city's years of expensive storm-mitigation efforts had actually paid off. The assassin climbed over the barriers first, his hand in his jacket.

The two figures stepped forward, their features swimming from the murk. The tall and cadaverous one in the long purple raincoat was obviously an assistant or bodyguard of some sort, and she recognized the other, squat one as Max, but...

Well, Max had something over his face. A mask composed of mirror shards. As they approached, he said, with a slight accent, "Keep your phones in your pockets."

"Done," Fiona said. "Thanks for meeting with us."

"You are very lucky I live up the street." Max removed his mask, revealing a squarish blonde head, his thin mouth framed by a slight goatee. Despite the rain, he was dressed in a beautiful blue suit with some kind of silver piping. As they approached, she saw the piping was composed of little symbols—tiny Bitcoin icons, each of them no doubt hand-stitched at considerable expense.

"The boat's just up there, Anthony is your captain," Max said. "As Bill knows, he's a good friend. He's very capable, as he just proved by riding out the storm to this point. But it's going to cost you."

"Fine."

A massive wave sloughed against the concrete walkway to their left, cresting in a towering burst of spray that almost reached the concrete barrier behind them. The finger-flick of an angry ocean. Fiona felt more than a little doubt about this operation. But what choice did they have?

"What are you supposed to be?" the assassin asked Max. "An escapee from the Matrix?"

"I actually represent a much longer and more distinguished line of cultural thought," Max offered, his spine stiffening. "One that extends back to William Gibson and the publication of 'Neuromancer,' and projects forward to a new future embracing web three, extensive shifting of digital ownership, and a radical reimagining of the blockchain. Sartorially speaking, I'm trying to show how cryptocurrency and Bitcoin—"

The assassin raised a hand. "Sorry, I have this medical condition, it makes me draw the nearest firearm whenever I hear the word 'Bitcoin.'"

Fiona eyed Max's bodyguard, who had crouched slightly,

his forearm inside his ridiculous jacket. In a true gunfight, this slab of rent-a-muscle would have been vaporized before his weapon left the holster. She cocked an eyebrow at him: *Relax, buddy. It's okay.*

The bodyguard pouted a bit as he straightened up, his hands returning to his sides. She made a mental note to recommend a few good mercenary services to Max before the week was out.

Max, regaining some of his composure, said, "I do not understand, I was just discussing how Bit..."

"Ah, yep, I feel it happening," the assassin's right hand made a long, exaggerated dip toward his hip. "I really should have a doctor check it out, but it also means I don't have to listen to any more conversations about stupid online currency, so, I guess that's a good thing?"

Max coughed into his hand. He was trying so hard to stay calm, but his fingers trembled. She almost felt sorry for the dude, except she knew his personal stash of cryptocurrency had made him a gazillionaire, provided the internet didn't wake up one day and decide all those bits were worthless.

"Can we get this done?" she said.

"Certainly," Max said, gesturing to the bodyguard, who stepped toward the railing, where two plastic crates awaited. Snapping open the top of the first one, he stepped back. Fiona spied four assault rifles set in foam.

"Satisfied?" Max asked.

"Next crate," Fiona said.

Max nodded and moved to the second crate, opening it to reveal a stack of black bullet-resistant vests and three helmets. He set those on the pavement so they could see the armaments nestled in foam at the bottom: two rows of extended magazines, along with a half-dozen grenades and two nylon pouches roughly the size of bread loaves. He yanked one of the pouches free and tossed it to Fiona, who caught it in mid-air and unzipped it.

"That is GPNVG," Max said, with a hint of pride. "Worth more than everything else in these crates combined."

Fiona pulled out a pair of night vision goggles with four lenses at the end of stubby stalks. "Where'd you find these? Gray market?"

"No, ma'am, that technology is commercial now. Costs as much as a car, but you get a ninety-degree field of view, focus from a foot to infinity, thirty hours' battery life."

"Okay," Fiona zipped the goggles into the pouch, which she tossed back. Drawing the titanium credit card from her pocket, she said: "You take plastic?"

Max smirked and shook his head.

"Oh, this isn't just any plastic. This is plastic that will change your life," Fiona said, her voice oddly musical—channeling Bill's conman hustle. "Belongs to a billionaire in Midtown who doesn't realize it's gone. I bet you can get three, maybe four times the value of these guns before it gets shut down."

Max hissed through his teeth. "Billionaires like tracking down anyone who rips them off."

"Very true." Fiona grinned, holding out the card at arm's length. "But this billionaire just happens to be running from the law, so he doesn't exactly have time to check his statements. Trust me, I've been using it for a week with no issues. I bet a smart boy like you can figure it out."

"Fine," Max snatched the card from her, tapping a fingernail against its luxurious metal. "But if I don't get fair value from this, I'm going to want Bit..."

"Sure. Cold, hard cash. Did I mention we're cutting you in, whatever we find on the island?"

"So Bill told me. But you're going to have to do the digging yourself. We're just in the supply and transport business." Pocketing the card, Max drew his geometric mask and slipped it over his lower face. His bodyguard already backing away.

Once they disappeared into the whistling darkness, Fiona turned to the assassin. "Let's get this shit on the boat."

Wonder of wonders, the crates featured wheels and handles. It made the work of dragging them down the wet pier and onto the boat a little easier. Onboard, the deck rolled in the vicious current. If it was this bad while the boat was still tied up at the dock, how well would they fare on a high-speed jaunt across the water?

Through the humid window, Anthony jerked and dipped as he readied for launch. The engine cycled up, the water frothing behind the boat. Beyond the bow, they had a better view of the channel separating Manhattan from North Brother Island, churning with whitewater. The ocean popped and crackled and roared. It wanted to kill everyone.

Fiona tapped the cockpit window. "We better get going," she said.

The cockpit door opened wide enough for Anthony to poke his head through, his brow knotted in concentration. He looked like a refugee from the 19th century, his enormous muttonchops threatening to swallow his thin cheeks. "Cast off," he said. "Then tie down. Not my problem if your ass goes sailing off the back."

"Any life vests on this thing?" the assassin asked.

Anthony chuckled before slamming the door again.

Fiona untethered the boat from the dock and sat down.

Her stomach felt as if she'd swallowed down a couple shots of horseradish vodka along with a couple pints of beer, and she clenched her throat to hold back any vomit.

"We might be about to die," the assassin offered.

"What else is new?" Fiona said.

With a massive jolt, the boat bumped away from the pier, rising on a swell as it did so. Infinite tons of oceanwater rumbling on the other side of the hull, more than capable of crushing them in an instant. Try to ignore it, she told herself. Concentrate instead on the army of gunmen waiting for you on a remote island.

22

IN THE BRONX, the water on the street rose to maybe mid-axle on the APC, but if the vehicle had a mouth, it would have laughed merrily as it splashed through. Beyond the small portholes Bill caught flashes of the ocean's titanic churn, an infinity of white waves battering the shore.

By the time they reached the boat, the eye was overhead, the rain settling to a light drizzle. Soul Patch kept a pistol pointed at Bill's spine as they boarded the enormous police launch bristling with lights, its engine rumbling. Bill, never the world's biggest fan of water, braced himself in a sheltered portion of the deck as the rest of the cops talked by the bow.

At least they hadn't taken on reinforcements. Whoever was piloting the boat stayed in the cabin far above, any crewmen remaining below. As they powered across the water, North Brother was a black hole within the deeper night.

After so many weeks of planning his own raid on the island, he was a bit unimpressed by its size.

They had some trouble tying up on the crumbling concrete jetty that jutted from North Brother's western edge like a diseased tongue. The boat slowed as it neared, churning the water to a misty froth. A monster swell lifted them with such force that Bill heard Soul Patch bark a startled curse before they slammed down again.

The bow crunched against the jetty. A spotlight found a patch of uncracked concrete. Tattoo mounted the railing with a rope in his hand, paused as the boat dipped, and jumped, suspended over the water for a queasy second before hitting the wet concrete and rolling, rising to his feet, tying off one rope to a rusted cleat, then sprinting a few feet to catch and tie up the other rope tossed to him from the deck.

They were secure against the jetty but the ocean was determined to smash them apart. Swells crashing against the hull hard enough to set lights swinging, metal groaning. "Let's go," Soul Patch said, hauling Bill to his feet.

"Unlock my cuffs?" Bill asked. "I'll jump better."

Soul Patch snorted.

"Come on," Bill said. "Where the hell am I going to go, anyway?"

"You'll be all right," Soul Patch said, guiding him to the portion of the deck where the other cops had assembled, waiting for their individual moments to jump. They hit the concrete, groaning and cursing.

As he waited for his turn, Bill examined the sky. In the furthest distance, the horizon flickered with the occasional lightning flash from what he assumed was the wall of the hurricane's eye. Two hours, maybe, and the storm would rumble through again—

"Move," Soul Patch announced, shoving Bill to the deck railing. The boat dipped again, the jetty looming, and Bill leapt into space. Someone darted forward to catch him, but he landed on his outstretched hands, his knee skimming rough concrete. The ocean burst through the shrinking gap between hull and jetty, soaking him anew.

Two duffel bags crashed onto the jetty beside him, followed by Soul Patch and Crew Cut. Tattoo scrambled to untie the heaving boat while the rest followed their flashlights inland, dragging the duffel bags.

"Wait," Hardaway said, pointing at the boat. "Where the hell's he going?"

"Doesn't want to stay here," Tattoo called, hurling the ropes back over the railing. "Water's too rough."

"We'll radio them," Crew Cut said. "Won't take long for them to come back."

"If the storm doesn't hit first," Bill said.

"Shut up and move," Soul Patch snapped at him, gripping Bill's collar in his left hand while flicking on the enormous flashlight in his right. The other cops falling into line behind them. At the end of the jetty, they maneuvered onto a muddy road cutting through thick brush, the tall trees shaking and rustling in the wind. A few branches had fallen in the mud, but nothing they couldn't climb over.

Once they were a few yards away from the shore, with the brush acting as a windbreak, Soul Patch squeezed Bill's shoulder. Bill stopped. It was a truism of living in New York City that you never experienced true darkness, because every street featured approximately a billion lights. But out here, on this little spit of rock poking into Long Island Sound, the night was total, the only light coming from the cops' flashlights slicing the black.

Soul Patch nodded to Tattoo, who knelt and unzipped one of the duffel bags, pulling out what looked like one of those nylon-sleeved chains all the bike messengers used to lock up their rides. The chain had a massive padlock at one end, but there was something odd about it, a bit of brighter metal soldered onto the body, plus a tangle of wires wrapped around the shackle.

"Hold him still," Tattoo said.

Soul Patch tightened his grip on Bill's shoulder.

"What the hell is that?" Bill asked, trying to keep his tone light and conversational.

"Insurance," Tattoo said. "Gimme more light."

Leaning close, Hardaway shone her light on the padlock. The nylon sheath was lumpy, uneven. It didn't look like there was a chain under there at all. Shark twisted one of the wires on the shackle, and a small red light popped to life on the lock's underside.

Tattoo told Bill: "This is a collar bomb, and before you panic like a little bitch, just keep in mind it's totally safe until it's not."

"Okay," Bill said.

"This is going around your neck," Tattoo said. "You do anything—and I mean anything—that pisses us off, I hit a button and your head becomes a cloud, understand?"

"I hate to appear contradictory," Bill said, "but won't that also blow up anyone standing too close?"

Tattoo grinned, "Nah. The force is directed upward, through your head. Don't worry, hotshot, we've done this before. Got a guy to rob a bank while wearing one of them."

"What happened to that guy?"

"Let's just say he'll never need a hat again." Soul Patch chuckled.

"Hold still," Tattoo said, and draped the coil around Bill's neck, looping it twice, the rough nylon scraping his skin. The sheath was heavy against his chest. The open lock tapped against his sternum.

Tattoo slotted the metal loop at the coil's free end into the lock and snapped it shut. A loud beep. Bill flinched.

"Give me the detonator," Crew Cut said, and Tattoo tossed him a plastic lump, like the fob you might use to start a car. Crew Cut caught it in midair and slipped it into his pocket.

"Lead the way," Crew Cut told Bill.

Bill swallowed, the pebbled nylon rubbing against his throat. If this thing went off, would he feel anything? Or would his reality simply snap to black, like a television set when you yanked the cord?

"It's this way," he told them, gesturing down the path into the interior of the island. On the way across the channel, he had spotted two pillars, no more than slightly deeper lines against the sky: the exhaust stacks of the old power plant squatting on the island's southern coast. Smack-dab in the middle of the island, meanwhile, was the wreck of the old hospital, a couple stories of crumbling brick and missing floors and shattered windows.

As Soul Patch shoved him along the narrow road between the whispering trees, his shoes sucking at the mud, one of the cop's flashlights skimmed the brush lining the shore. Bill spied something useful: A small fiberglass boat, its hull barely visible between the branches and thorns. The flashlight swung away before Bill could see whether it had an outboard motor. Even so. Someone, maybe a Parks employee, might have dragged it onshore before the storm hit. If it worked, it could provide a way off this rock.

But first, Bill needed to figure out how to get rid of these cops without getting his head blown off. He had no clear plan, but the hospital presented good opportunities to improvise. Lots of corridors and empty rooms. Lots of thick brick walls that might block a signal from a detonator to an explosive collar. And hopefully a sharp instrument or two. He knew how to stab.

23

IN A LIFE sprinkled liberally with all kinds of bad ideas, deciding to take a boat across Long Island Sound in the middle of a fierce hurricane was going to rank near the top—if they lived. Fiona crouched on the deck, soaked by the swells splashing over the railing, shivering despite her layers of waterproof clothing.

Anthony at the helm seemed to know what he was doing, tacking so they faced the swells head-on. It was like riding a roller-coaster, the boat powering up the face of the swell for a few seconds before rumbling down the far side, the bow colliding with the trough hard enough to lash them with cold, blinding spray.

She hoped with all her heart Bill was still alive.

A slithering of nylon on steel, a cough, and her friend the assassin was next to her, crouching against the hull. "Just like old times, huh?" he said.

She shook her head. "I've never been on a boat with you."

"No, I meant heading into battle." He paused as another swell smashed over the bow, dousing them with cold water. "That lunatic's farm in Oklahoma. The barn. All those rednecks wanting our heads on their walls."

"This is nothing like that," she said.

The assassin clapped her on the shoulder. "Just don't shoot me again," he said. He was smiling but his eyes were cold. "I'm down to one kidney, one ball, and, like, six inches of small intestine. No, I'm kidding. Or am I?"

She put her hand on his, meaning to push it away—and paused. Squeezed his cold fingers. "I'm sorry for shooting you," she said.

His smile widened, his teeth flickering in the dimness. "I sure hope so."

Another wave and fist of cold spray, another opportunity for her to take a deep breath and think, really think, back to Oklahoma, the barn on fire and the fields around the farmhouse strewn with bodies and parts of bodies, and how heavy the smoking rifle felt in her hand as she aimed it at the white gleam of the assassin's back—

"No, I mean it," she said. "I've felt terrible about it ever since."

Another wave, unexpected, smashed over them. The boat's motors whining as Anthony adjusted course. She was suddenly overcome by the urge to stand up and check where they were in relation to North Brother, but the black holes of the assassin's eyes rooted her to the deck.

"I've always wondered why you did it in the first place," he said.

"I don't know," she said. "Trust issues, maybe?"

He coughed, or maybe it was a snort. "Trust issues."

"If you knew me, it would make sense," she offered, compelled like few other times in her life to explain more, but at that moment Anthony killed the running lights. The only illumination came from a red light inside the pilot's cabin as Fiona rose to her knees to peer over the railing.

North Brother Island maybe a hundred yards ahead now, silhouetted against the deeper night. The engine coughed, died. Inside the cabin, Anthony's silhouette extended an arm, finger tapping the glass of the port-side window.

She rose a little higher, following the direction of Anthony's finger to the island's flank. In the darkness, a glimmer—a boat rumbling its way across the channel toward the Bronx.

"That's them," the assassin said, more of a statement than a question.

"We should get ready," she said, crab-walking to the locker beside the assassin and opening it. She pulled out the backpack with the grenades and night-vision gear and slung it over her shoulder. Next, she took one of the rifles, grateful they were heading into battle so well-armed. Could you imagine trying to take on a bunch of crooked cops with just a knife or a pistol or something? You might as well pray for death—

An awesome crunch—ear-splitting, body-crushing, world-ending. Her body spun, weightless as the boat rose beneath them, wood splintering, metal flying, lights sparking. Cold ocean smashing her in the face, robbing her of breath, lifting her toward the stars. She had a bird's view of the ship beneath her, its spine broken, the deck opening like a jagged mouth, the assassin tumbling over the railing into the foaming swells, and for a lunatic instant she imagined she might keep drifting upwards, away from all this insanity, but then gravity gripped her by the wet ankles and she was spiraling down again, back to the water in the time it took to blink, so fast she barely had time to throw her arms in front of her face and take a breath and squeeze her eyes shut. Her instincts told her to swim away from the dying boat before it sucked down everything around it, and she kicked as hard as she could but her boots were too heavy, dragging her legs down, so she had to pause and work her numb fingers between the laces and pull, pull, pull until one boot yanked free, and she set to work on the other but her lungs were burning, she was about to die but no, the boot was off and she kicked for the surface, sucking down cold air crackling with foam, oxygen filling her with life, her vision and hearing snapping into focus.

Thrashing in the water, she looked around.

The boat was gone.

The assassin was gone.

Her guns were gone.

The backpack with the grenades and night-vision goggles was gone.

Her shoes, phone, wallet—all of it headed for the bottom of Long Island Sound.

She needed to swim as hard as she could for the black island where men with guns awaited her. At least the current carried her in the right direction. She could angle her body and ride it toward the faint swath of rocky beach.

To her right, a shout—the assassin splashing in her direction, soaking wet but strong enough to swim. He was alive, at least, but she bet Anthony was dead.

Her knees scraped rock. She sank her fingers deep into mud and pulled herself forward, coughing out seawater and stinging vomit. She crawled across the beach until she was well past the breakers and sank down, her forehead resting on her knees. Every part of her ached—not an unfamiliar feeling. As she focused on her breathing, she made a list in her head:

Find shoes.

Find a gun.

Find Bill.

And if Bill says so much as one sarcastic word to you, slap the almighty shit out of him.

24

THE HOSPITAL LOOMED, three stories of vine-covered brick lined with shattered windows. The storm had uprooted several of the larger trees in front. Bill climbed over the trunks, the rough bark snagging his sodden suit pants, the explosive belt tapping against his collarbone.

When he reached the far side of the treefall, he turned to watch the other cops struggling over the trees. He almost offered a hand to help Crew Cut. If the man tripped and fell wrong, it might set off the detonator in his pocket, and wouldn't that be a hilarious and awful way to go?

Once on the hospital side of the pile, the cops had to pause to suck down oxygen. None of them were in good shape, especially with thick mud sucking at their feet with every step. Their clothes already pricked and torn by the thorny bushes growing waist-high along the path from the jetty to here. *Get weaker,* Bill told them in his mind. *Get slower, get dumber.*

People could mock the power of positive thinking all they wanted, but he figured it couldn't hurt at this juncture.

Crew Cut flicked his light across the front of the hospital. A short flight of stairs led onto a crumbling concrete terrace and the jagged hole of the hospital's front doorway. To Bill's overactive imagination, it looked like a monster's mouth.

"Lead the way," Hardaway said, her grip tightening on the shovel in her hands. "You don't have much time."

"None of us do," Bill said, smiling into the flashlight's blinding beam.

Now comes the tricky part, Bill thought. I'm all out of tricks. I've spent tonight trying to buy time—all for nothing. If this was a con, and it wasn't going well, this would be the opportunity to slip out the back. Alas, no such option on an island. Not when you're surrounded by people like this.

"Move it," Shark said.

Bill stepped through the doorway. The flashlights illuminated an oval room, broad window-frames with wooden benches on either side. The ceiling and its ornate molding chipped and cracking in places, the floor piled high with chunks of paint and plaster. A few dusty chairs and a tipped-over cart in one corner. From his internet research, he knew this was the lobby of the Tuberculosis Pavilion, where patients could cough their lungs out in relative isolation. Typhoid Mary had died here, right?

Tattoo swept his flashlight in a circle, huge corridors disappearing into the murk. The ceiling of the Pavilion, still largely intact, had spared the room from the wrath of the storm, but Bill heard rushing water, along with a distressed creaking that could have been anything—trees scraping against the walls, soggy floors threatening to give way.

"To the right," Bill said, anticipating Crew Cut's next question.

"What's that way?"

"Stairs to the basement," Bill said. "One guy told me it's buried down there, below an old iron lung."

"You believed him?"

Bill shrugged. "Good a place to start as any."

They took the right corridor, the cops' flashlights playing over rusted spiral staircases leading to higher floors, wet brick walls covered in moss and the stark slashes of graffiti. The ceiling had collapsed in places, strewing piles of rubble everywhere. Bill tested each new step before committing his weight, fearful as he envisioned the floor crumbling.

They arrived at an intersection. On the wall to their right, a rusted metal sign, torn in half, announced 'Base—'. Their flashlights, shining through the doorway, swept over a spiral staircase curling into nothingness. The stair risers more rust than metal. Bill wondered whether it would hold more than a few pounds of anyone's weight.

"Yeah, you're leading off," Crew Cut told Bill.

"Keep that light on me," Bill said, stepping to the head of the stairs. He toed the first riser. With a terrible groan, the staircase shifted an inch to the left. Rust rained into the abyss.

Holding his breath, Bill settled his weight more firmly.

Nothing happened.

Both feet now. He stood there, craning his head for a view beyond the staircase into the void below. From this angle, Crew Cut's flashlight cut off at a black line maybe ten feet further down.

Bill took the next step. The riser creaked but held.

Drops of water glittered in the flashlight beams. It sounded like it was raining down here.

Another step. Above him, Crew Cut shifted positions so he could shine the light past Bill to the bottom of the staircase. The light played over muddy water maybe three or four feet deep. Paint chips and bark and leaves floated in it, carried by a powerful current into a maze of rooms.

Crew Cut cursed.

"We might as well check the other spots," Bill said, hoping their desperation wouldn't push them into descending any further. Even if the money was down here, buried beneath some massive piece of machinery, there was no way they could dig it up.

Crew Cut sighed. "Right."

Bill took his time on the ascent, the staircase shuddering with his every movement. It was sweet relief when his feet reached the top again. Back to the corridor, where a fresh burst of wind scattered a storm of wet leaves and plaster bits. For the first time, Bill noticed how the exterior wall had collapsed at the end of the corridor to the right. The hole framed the dripping woods to the island's south; on a clear day, you would have seen Manhattan's skyscrapers piercing the sky in the distance. With the grid down, the world was shadows—except for fifty yards distant, deep in the brush, where an orange flame spat sparks into the wind.

"What the hell?" Tattoo said.

25

I'D BEEN THROUGH a lot in the past several months. Getting shot in the back while wearing an Elvis costume. Stealing a car from a serial killer. Trying to figure out how to use my limited skills to pay for a New York apartment, a task that placed me in unfortunate proximity with someone nicknamed the Lube King. But almost drowning was perhaps the capstone humiliation of it all, if only because there was no way for my brain to rationalize or make a joke out of it.

When you plunge into the ocean, cold water rushing down your nose and throat and filling your lungs, your panicked lizard brain wipes out all conscious thought. You become a jerking puppet, all reactions, nothing but panic.

Fortunately, the saner part of my brain—what little of it was left—managed to assert control after a few seconds. I needed buoyancy or I was going to sink straight to the bottom, where I should rot forever among the discarded gun parts and rusted cars littering the bottom of Long Island Sound.

I kicked off my shoes.

I stripped off my jacket.

I'd already lost my gun.

Opening my eyes in the stinging murk, I spied a faint trail of bubbles from my mouth streaming upward. I lashed my body that way, crashing above the surface as a fresh wave smashed me in the face. At least I was only a few yards from the island's rocky shore.

I spied the faint shape of Fiona crawling ashore and kicked for her as hard as I could. The current tugged at my legs, threatening to pull me away, but within a few yards I passed a massive pile of concrete and rusted metal half-submerged in the surf. It blocked the worst of the waves, and after another few moments of paddling my feet scraped the bottom.

I stood.

Ashore, Fiona crouched behind a leaning trunk of a tree. This side of the island was all thick brush and stubby trees. Impossible to see far inland. I stumbled toward her, and my bare foot rammed against something hard and wet. I looked down. It was one of the backpacks from the boat.

Excellent. Things were finally looking up—which guns were in here? But when I unzipped the pack, I found only a few flares, a first aid kit, and a collapsible shovel with a dull blade. With the shovel in my left hand, I zipped the pack closed again.

"The boat's just gone," Fiona said.

"We must have hit something big," I said. "I'm betting Anthony's dead." I felt a little bad about the guy, but he also knew the risks. The last ride is always the greatest. How the hell were we going to get off this miserable rock?

"We should move," she said. "We'll freeze otherwise."

"Yeah, but where?"

She nodded. "Based off Bill's maps, the hospital is up and to our right, I think. It's the biggest structure on the island. I bet they'll head there first."

"And then?"

"And then what?"

"That's what I'm asking you," I said. "In case you didn't notice, we don't have guns. We don't even have shoes. Just some flares and a first-aid kit in this stupid pack. By the way, if I'm killed, I want you to launch my ashes into space on one of those rockets. Leave this shit-box completely—"

"Aren't you a badass assassin?" she said. "Isn't that a shovel in your hand? We'll improvise."

"You have a point," I said. "You know, one time I was stuck in this bar in Mexico, surrounded by these cartel dudes, and I only had a toothpick—"

"I'm sure it's an interesting story that ends with you yanking out a dude's liver with your teeth," she said, moving around the tree, careful to step on larger stones and avoid the brush. "But something tells me we need to hurry."

Once we punched inland, it was much easier going. Thick trees, their trunks wrapped in ivy, lined up with pleasing symmetry as we passed through shin-high grass. Even before my feet touched brick beneath a thin layer of mud, I realized we were on a road only partially swallowed up by nature. The dim shapes of buildings to our left and right. How many people had once lived on this island?

How many ghosts live here now?

Okay, Mister Melodramatic. You're crazy enough without jumping at shadows like a virgin in a Victorian horror novel. Fiona drifted to the left, attempting to use the thicker trees as a screen from whatever might lie ahead, and I followed. The storm had knocked down crazy tangles of branches, so many it was impossible to avoid cracking over one or two, the noise loud as gunshots over the wind whispering through the trees.

Fiona paused and raised a fist. I stopped behind her.

She pointed ahead, toward a clearing, beyond it the hulk of a huge building. The thin white lines of flashlights slicing against the darkness: a group heading up the stone steps toward the crumbled remains of a pavilion. Even at this distance, I recognized Bill, dressed in a gray suit, with a thick and shiny necklace around his neck—a restraint of some sort? I didn't recognize any of the people with him.

"Tactical nightmare," I whispered, nodding at the building. "Unless you want to play movie slasher, try to pick them off one by one?"

"Let me guess, you've done something like that?"

I snorted. "Of course not. That's why the mask-wearing slasher in those movies is always invulnerable to bullets—otherwise they'd be dead in the first five minutes."

"Come up with a better idea." Fiona squinted at the group as the last of them disappeared inside. "I leave Bill alone for a couple of hours and he gets into this shit."

"Welcome to marriage." I raised one of my feet, twisting it for a better look at the sole. During the trek inland, I had stepped on a few burrs or twigs, but nothing felt like it had penetrated the skin—or so I thought, until I saw the blood smeared on my skin. If we were going to make it much farther, we would need something to cover our feet.

Shrugging out of my rainproof jacket, I hooked the edge of the shovel into the sleeve and pulled until the fabric ripped. Repeated the action at three other spots, dividing the sleeve into four pieces of jagged cloth.

"Put these around your feet," I said, tossing her two of the strips. "It's not exactly a pair of Nike trainers, but it might protect your skin a little."

"Smart," she said, wrapping her feet.

As I clinched waterproof nylon over my aching soles, I examined the area around us. A low brick structure to our right, maybe a shed of some kind. Time and weather had demolished two of its walls into piles of brick, revealing a concrete foundation piled with years' worth of branches, wet leaves, and rubble. I skittered that way, stepping as carefully as I could over the remains of the outer wall.

I peeled back a few of the larger branches atop the pile, revealing the tangle of wood chips and bark and assorted crap. Moist, but not soaking wet. From the backpack, I extracted one of the flares and scraped it to life, red flames and smoke blooming from its tip. The heat felt good on my wet skin. Fiona made wordless sounds of protest behind me, but I didn't care. I shoved the sparking flare deep into the pile and returned to the brush, doing my best to suppress a grin.

"What's the point of that?" she asked. "You just like setting fires?"

"Think about it and it'll come to you," I said.

The flare ignited the wood. Thick smoke poured from the shed. The surviving walls blocked some of the wind, giving the flames a better chance to take hold.

Fiona nodded. "Oh, okay."

"Right?"

"You want to stay here?"

"Let's get back a bit," I said, nodding behind us. "If they come in force and spread out, I want a little more space."

"More left," she said, pointing at a thicker patch of brush. "Room to hide."

As we scuttled low, I picked up a thick piece of brick in the path. We had shoddy weapons at our disposal, but we were professionals, right? We knew how to use cover. We would hide out at the intersection of a low brick wall and the overhanging trees, waiting like tigers until our idiotic prey wandered too close.

I held onto that vision for another three minutes, until the first rifle-shot blasted apart a branch six inches above my head.

Someone screamed in the distance. I couldn't pick out the words over the wind. Based on how Fiona's face tightened with fear as we hit the mud, I bet it was Bill.

26

THE FLAME REMINDED Bill of the old stories his grand-mama used to tell him about will o' wisps in the swamp, burning spirits that led the unsuspecting to their doom. A perfect thought for a haunted setting like this.

"Lightning?" Hardaway asked.

"What?" Crew Cut pressed himself against a wall.

"Like, lightning set something on fire over there," Hardaway said. "There can't be anyone else on this island, can there?"

"Sure, just some dude in a hockey mask with a machete," Tattoo said, and giggled. "He's been on this island here for-ever. And he's really happy we're here."

"Shut the fuck up," Soul Patch said, kneeling to unzip the massive duffel bag at his feet. "There's a quick way to figure this out."

"Oh shit," Crew Cut said, sounding elated. "You bring the thermal?"

"Hell yeah I did," Soul Patch said. From the bag he drew out a long bundle of waterproof fabric, which he unrolled on the wet floor, revealing the parts of a rifle. He assembled the weapon with expert precision, then clipped on a bipod and an oversized scope. Bill guessed the man could do it blindfolded.

Soul Patch lowered the rifle to the floor and settled himself behind it, peering through the scope's eyepiece.

"What's that?" Bill asked.

"It's a thermal scope," Crew Cut said. "If there's anything out there larger than an ant, the scope will pick it up."

"Got two shapes," Soul Patch said, adjusting his stance slightly. "Looks like people. To the right of the fire, maybe ten yards."

"What are they doing?" Tattoo asked. Kneeling beside Crew Cut, he reached into the bag and extracted a double-barreled shotgun, sawed off close to the stock. Breaking the weapon open revealed two shells. He snapped it closed again and retreated to the wall.

Soul Patch squinted. "Staying still. One of them has what maybe looks like a backpack or something. I don't see any weapons."

"Anyone from Parks on this island?" Hardaway said, pressing herself against the wall beside Crew Cut. "Someone riding out the storm, maybe?"

"Maybe, but that doesn't make sense. They had plenty of time to evacuate." Crew Cut's head swiveled, his gaze finding Bill. "You have anything to tell us?"

"No idea," Bill said, wondering if he should take cover. Was it Fiona out there? He was tempted to ask Soul Patch if one of the figures was a woman, which might give too much away. If it was Fiona, who did she bring with her?

"What do we do?" Soul Patch said.

"What we have to," Crew Cut retorted.

Soul Patch titled his head away from the scope, squinting up at the older cop. "What do you mean?"

"You know what I mean. No witnesses."

And in the space between heartbeats, Bill knew it was her out there. She had come for him, somehow. She had pieced together his garbled messages and made her way through the storm and now she was readying to rain hellfire down on these chumps who had captured him, because that was how this shit worked, they were on a telepathic level that had allowed them to survive again and again, more than the sum of their parts, only she didn't know about the cop in the shadows with the sniper rifle and the thermal scope—

"No witnesses," Crew Cut said again. "I'm sorry, but that's just the way it goes. Bad luck they were out here tonight."

Hardaway looking at Bill now, evaluating him in the same way as Crew Cut. "You sure you don't have anything to tell us?"

Bill shook his head. "I swear, I don't know what's going on."

His eye fixed to the scope, Soul Patch loaded the rifle, worked the bolt. "This really sucks," he said. "It's a man and a woman. They're crouched down, waiting."

"You didn't have to tell me that," Crew Cut said.

"Yes, I did," Soul Patch said, seating the rifle more firmly against his shoulder. "You know, we have all the firepower. We can just go down there, tie them up. There's no reason to add two more bodies to our fuckin' ledger."

"We do have rope," Tattoo said.

It's her, Bill thought. She's out there, and they're about to put a bullet in her head. Maybe I can grab the rifle and run, take a left through the doorway over there. They won't expect it. The guy with the shotgun won't fire because he'll fear hitting one of his friends, and the rest don't have their guns out. I can make it, right?

No, of course not. Because he had this explosive collar around his neck, its cold weight pressing his skin, and Crew Cut had the detonator. He might only make it fifteen feet before the cop pressed a button and splattered the walls with his brains.

"Move over," Crew Cut said, looming above Soul Patch, who stared at him for a long moment before rolling away. Crew Cut knelt behind the rifle and placed his eye to the scope.

Fuck it, Bill thought. I was always the weaker of the two of us, anyway. Sorry, babe. Would've been nice to spend another morning in bed with you.

He lashed out his right foot at the rifle's barrel. He underestimated the distance, but his reach was long enough. His toe scraped the edge of the stock, bumping the rifle a few inches to the left as Crew Cut's finger tightened on the trigger.

An ear-quaking boom as the rifle fired.

Bits of plaster rained from the ceiling.

Bill primed his foot for another kick, ready to deny Crew Cut a second shot, but Hardaway's forearm wrapped around his neck, her other hand on the back of his skull, her foot slamming into his shin hard enough to drive him into the ground, but in mid-fall he had enough time and breath to shout: *"FIONA, RUN."*

So much for famous last words. He hit the floor, knocking the remaining air from his lungs, Hardaway spinning around to drop a knee on his chest. This was it—but what did he expect? Most criminals died under terrible circumstances, in terrible places. Why should he have bucked the odds?

Instead of adjusting the rifle and firing another shot, Crew Cut was on his feet, scrambling his pistol free from its holster, his face red with rage. "The fuck," he wheezed between clenched teeth, cocking the hammer of his weapon back. "You fucked with me for the last time."

It was worth it, Bill wanted to say—better last words, if only he had the air to form them.

27

FIONA'S HAND SLAPPED her hip, a reflex toward a nonexistent pistol. The assassin already scrambling away from her, deeper into the brush. She followed, doing her best to keep the larger trees between her and the hospital. The first shot had vaporized the branch over their heads, peppering them with sap and wood-chips, which meant it was a high-powered rifle—whoever these fuckers were, they came ready to fight World War III.

"Night vision or thermal," the assassin said, crawling on hands and knees. Fiona tensed, expecting a second shot to blow her head clean off—

Nothing but the moaning wind and dripping water.

What was going on?

From the direction of the hospital, a loud crash. It sounded like metal slapping metal. No round whistled overhead. Was it a gunshot? Or something else?

God, she hoped Bill was okay.

"We're no good out here," the assassin said, rising behind a thick tree. "Oh shit, I dropped the shovel somewhere."

If those people inside the hospital had night-vision goggles or a special scope, they had all the advantages. They could set up a position and plug away until they scored hits or the hurricane roared back in, whichever came first.

Fiona rose to a crouch. Bill had showed her the maps of the island more than a few times, but to be honest, she had tuned out most of what he was saying. It was one of those relationship things: your partner falls in love with something and prattles on about it endlessly, and sooner or later you begin to smile and nod and think about something else— anything else—whenever the topic comes up. She remembered him talking about the sites where the money could possibly be buried, including...

"There's a lighthouse," she said. "It should be straight up and to the right from here. Not far from the hospital."

"You want to trap us in an enclosed space?"

"Better than staying out in the open. We can set an ambush."

"With what? A fucking rock and a smile?" the assassin said, bending down to pull at some wet vines, revealing a rusted length of rebar. He hefted it, judging the balance. "Think this will scare them?"

"Anything's a weapon if you're creative enough," she said. "Let's go."

She led off, moving as quickly as she dared.

Between the wind snapping between the trees overhead, the water pattering from the trees, and the roar of waves pounding the shore, it was impossible to hear the deeper sounds of the forest. If someone was sneaking up on them, they'd never know until it was too late.

Fiona had to tell herself the flickers of movement at the edges of her vision were only brush moving in the wind—only that and nothing more. Her eye kept trying to manifest figures, people stalking forward with oversized helmets on their heads and guns in their hands, and she had to breathe in, breathe out to stop her attack instincts from kicking in.

The brush grew so thick they were almost swimming through it. The rocky shore was to their left now, tantalizingly close, so much easier to travel along, but stepping out into the open would make them targets.

Beyond the roaring shoreline, flashes of lightning in the distance. Far side of the hurricane's eyewall approaching faster, more rain and lightning and skin-stripping wind beyond it. If they weren't off this island—somehow—by the time it hit, they would need to take cover somewhere until it passed.

If a piece of flying debris or rising floodwaters didn't kill them in the meantime.

Or a bunch of gunmen.

"Is that it?" whispered the assassin, pointing ahead of them.

Maybe fifty yards ahead to their left, atop a spit of muddy land jutting into the water: two stories of crumbled brick and rotted wood, barely held together by webs of thick vines and weeds. It looked more like a bunker than a stereotypical lighthouse, but maybe the upper floors had collapsed at some point over the past few decades. "That's it," Fiona said, redoubling her efforts to plunge through this damn brush.

Hopefully there would be something useful inside the aged wreck of the lighthouse. An iron bar, a rusty knife, anything with weight or an edge she could use.

Hopefully the floor or the ceiling wouldn't give way as soon as they stepped inside.

Hopefully Bill was still alive and breathing, because otherwise she didn't know what the hell she would do—

Flashlights in the trees to their right. At least three or four people, moving through the woods at speed. Fiona sped up on aching legs, the assassin breathing hard beside her.

28

CREW CUT'S PISTOL in his face, Bill wondering if this was it, the Big Adios—and then Hardaway snapped:

"Stop."

Crew Cut's eyes flicking toward her, brow furrowed in annoyance.

"We need him alive," Hardaway said, stepping to her left for a better look at startled Bill.

"This better be good," Tattoo chuckled.

"Fiona," Hardaway said, her eyes locked on Bill. "That's your girlfriend?"

Crew Cut leaned back, the weapon drifting away from Bill. The vein twitching on Crew Cut's brow said how much he wanted to pull that trigger.

"The task force, where we first learned about Bill here," Hardaway continued, and chuckled. "He was traveling with a woman, Fiona, I forget her last name but she was an enforcer for Rockaway, racked up a serious body count. Bill said he broke up with her, but that was a lie, wasn't it, Bill?"

"Yes," Bill said. Why lie at this juncture?

Crew Cut turned and lashed a foot at the wall. The brick imploded in a cloud of dust.

"I bet it's her," Hardaway said. "And if it is, we'll need a hostage. It'll make dealing with her a whole lot easier. Unless you want to spend the rest of the night playing cat and mouse with a super-killer?"

"You said there was someone with her?" Soul Patch asked. "Who's that?"

"Great, two killers," Tattoo offered. Setting down his shotgun, he retrieved the rifle, collapsed the bipod, and retreated to his former position against the wall. Squinting into the thermal scope, he scanned the woods beyond the hole. "I don't see them now."

Soul Patch deadpanned: "What else could go wrong."

"Screw it, okay, so they're out there." Crew Cut took a deep breath, his massive shoulders rising, and let it out slowly. "We're not abandoning this, do you understand? We've come too far."

"What's the next site?" Hardaway asked.

Bill tried to think. Two of the sites were out in the woods, down near the remains of an old dock. It was thick brush through there, with lots of opportunities for Fiona and whoever was with her to set up an ambush—but thanks to the thermal scope on the rifle, a sneak attack was impossible. That left one site with enough blind spots for Fiona to do her best work.

"The lighthouse," Bill said. "It's not far from here."

"Okay," Hardaway said. "And where do you think she'd go? Would she head there?"

"She's not stupid," Bill said. "You're a bunch of people with guns. She has no guns. She's not going to be trapped in a small space with you."

"Fine," Crew Cut said, waving for Tattoo to hand over the rifle. "Let's move right now."

As Crew Cut took the rifle, adjusting his grip so he held it at port arms, Bill thought: There's your first mistake, amigo. You need two hands to hold a sizable piece of masculinity-affirming hardware like that, and that's one fewer hand holding the detonator for this nuke around my neck. Maybe it would take you two seconds to set the rifle down and reach into your pocket, which isn't much time, but maybe it'll be all the time I need.

"Let's get this shit done," Soul Patch said, with the testosterone-fueled growl of an action hero in the movies he doubtlessly loved. Leading off, he stepped onto the pile of rubble at the base of the hole, scanning the ground beyond the hospital for threats. It would have been the perfect moment if Fiona had something planned for him—if not a bullet, certainly a brick thrown at high velocity—but he leapt through unharmed.

The rest followed. The lighthouse was to their right, beyond the muddy path they'd taken to reach the hospital. As they spread out behind Crew Cut, Hardaway slid into position behind Bill. He could hear her breathing hard, exhausted, anxious. Good.

The path ended in a wall of trees. Tattoo and Soul Patch clicked on their flashlights, the glow flaring the branches and brush into scattered patterns of brightness and shadow, a thousand phantom arms reaching for them—

Bill hoped their adrenaline was running high. If they were excited or scared, it would lead to mistakes. Maybe I can get my hands on that detonator, he thought, allowing himself the tiniest sip of hope. If I can do that, and get away from them, Fiona and whoever's with her can kill these fools. Even better, Fiona must have gotten here by boat.

Bill stopped in the middle of the muddy path, curious how Hardaway would react. She poked him in the small of his back with her pistol, but softly. "Move," she muttered.

"Whatever." He was right: she was tired. Excellent.

Past the line of trees, the silhouette of the lighthouse hulked against the bruised-purple sky. The dull crunch and snap of vegetation somewhere to their left. Maybe footsteps, maybe the wind. At the head of the pack, Soul Patch knelt in the mud, the rifle's scope raised to his eye, and cursed.

"What's going on?" Tattoo asked, stepping behind a thick tree to their right.

Crew Cut scanned the facade left to right, up and down. "Two shapes, I think. They're in there."

"It's them," Hardaway said.

"Thanks, Miss Obvious." Crew Cut shouted like he was trying to control a riot: *"You better come out! We got your boy as a hostage!"*

No reply from the building. Bill hoped she was preparing all kinds of nasty traps. I hope you rip them up, babe. Nobody does it better than you.

"Hardaway, Brooks," Crew Cut nodded at the doorway. "You're at bat."

"What?" Tattoo asked.

"Go the fuck in," Crew Cut said. "You got a pistol and a shotgun. Cut them apart. We'll cover you from outside. Then we dig."

29

A HUNDRED YEARS ago, the North Brother Island lighthouse must have been a beautiful example of minimalist architecture, with its solid brick walls and an iron spiral staircase ascending to the roof. But decades of salty air and storms had turned it into a haunted house—and Fiona and I were the ghosts.

We entered through a gaping hole in the rear wall. A wide doorway to our left, beyond the staircase, led to the building's front rooms. More than enough walls to protect us from their thermal scope or night-vision goggles.

The rusted remains of the staircase looked like the spine of an enormous creature twisting through a ragged hole in the roof. The faintest light trickling through the opening played over moss-coated bricks, a floor littered with stones and dirt and bits of litter.

Shouting from outside: *"You better come out! We got your boy as a hostage!"*

I glanced at Fiona. "He's alive, at least."

"For now," she said, scanning the floor as if a heavy- caliber machine gun might magically appear to even the odds for us.

No firearms were forthcoming, but I spotted a wooden handle, maybe two feet in length and broken with a jagged end. I snatched it up, hoping it wouldn't shatter if I hit something with it.

From the front rooms: a scrape, a crackle of rocks.

They were coming after us.

I gestured for Fiona to stand on the right side of the doorway. As she moved, I reached into the backpack and extracted one of the flares. Popped it to life. Hurled it as hard as I could up the staircase. My aim was true: the sputtering, flaring light landed on whatever was left of the floor above us, its red glow flickering against the shattered brick.

I trotted to the side of the doorway opposite Fiona. Even in the dark, I couldn't miss the look of utter disdain on her face. Yes, as an ambush, it sucked—what kind of slack-jawed moron would see a bright light and walk right toward it, assuming they'd find their prey there?

I wasn't trying for some Ulysses S. Grant-level subterfuge, though. I only needed a second of distraction.

The flare bought us that and more.

The crunch of feet on gravel. Someone murmured on the far side of the doorway, no more than ten or fifteen feet away. I worked my grip on the handle. Fiona had a rock in her hand.

The footsteps closed in.

I tensed, ready to spring.

The two figures darted into the room, moving fast and low, as if expecting a threat at the far end of the space. Maybe the flare's flickering glow destroyed their night vision a bit, too. The one closest to me was a heavyset dude with a square jaw, the bloody light playing over the snaking tattoo poking from the collar of his shirt. He gripped a sawed-off shotgun.

His partner was a woman, squarish and strong, her pistol leveled in a two-handed grip. She must have spied Fiona in her peripheral vision, because she began to turn in that direction—and Fiona, quick as a snake, brought the rock down on her head.

As she did, her partner turned toward the commotion— just as I slammed the handle down on his shotgun. At least, that's what I was aiming for. I intended to knock it from his hands, followed by a Babe Ruth swing for his face. Except my timing was off, the handle descending onto the hinge of his elbows, which snapped back, bringing the stubby barrels of the sawed-off to his face as his finger reflexively pulled the trigger.

Buckshot and bits of head splashed the wall. A cloud of brick dust drifting down. The woman yelled—she was already on the ground, Fiona's knees pinning her spine. Fiona had the woman's gun in one hand and was patting her down with the other. A wallet, a radio, a small knife hit the bricks.

My ears ringing, I retrieved the smoking shotgun and set it aside and patted the dead man's pockets until I found another few shells, a wallet, handcuffs, and a set of keys. I broke the shotgun open and reloaded, then flipped open the wallet to find the name of the man who'd just won Dumbest Death of the Year.

I stared at the badge and identification of an NYPD detective.

"Well, shit," I said. "That's a first for me, believe it or not."

Fiona looked over at the badge, then at the woman beneath her. "That's legit?"

"That's right," the woman said. "I'm Detective Hardaway, and you're in unbelievably deep shit. You surrender now and it might go a little better for you."

Fiona snorted. "Your friends outside, they're all cops, too?"

"Correct, Fiona," Hardaway said, flashing her teeth like a coyote stuck in a trap. "You're surrounded. We have Bill, too, so if you try anything stupid, he dies first."

"On a long enough timeline, we're all dead anyway," I said, tossing the handcuffs to her. "Better put those on."

"You know the drill," Fiona said, stepping off the cop, the cop's gun raised. "I got your weapon. Try anything funny, and..."

"Yeah, yeah, you'll do something terrible I won't live long enough to regret," Hardaway said, snapping the handcuffs over her wrists. "And look, I did these nice and tight, okay? I'm worth more to you alive."

"There are different degrees of 'alive,'" Fiona said.

Hardaway squinted at her. "I read your sheet when I was on the task force. Not a lot on you. But you put a lot of people down, didn't you?"

Hardaway's radio crackled: *"Hardaway? Report."*

"What should we have her say?" I asked.

"I won't say shit," Hardaway said.

"More might try to come in," I said. While Fiona dealt with Hardaway, I moved back to my former position in the doorway, doing my best to position my feet to avoid the spreading blood from what remained of the other cop's head. The shotgun blast would make anyone outside cautious about entering—for another minute or two, at least.

I trusted Fiona could watch the back windows and

Hardaway while I covered the front. The flare guttered its last above us, the black descending again like a curtain, and it took a few moments for my eyes to adjust. I spied the outline of the front door, a rectangle of slightly grayer murk.

Hardaway's radio crackled: *"Hardaway? Damn it, answer."*

I shrank back a little, anxious not to expose too much of my head to a thermal scope or night vision. I noticed something funny about the brick beside me.

When the unfortunate cop had cleared his mind, the buckshot had penetrated the wall's loose brick, knocking some of it loose to reveal a cavity. Something was in there. It looked like cloth.

I pulled a brick away. I pulled at another and another and another, opening a zigzag gap all the way to the floor—exposing three enormous duffel bags stacked atop one another.

"What you got?" Fiona whispered.

"Bags," I said, reaching for the top one—and stopped. The Dean had been a squirrely bugger, and smart. What's to say these bags didn't rest atop a pressure-activated mine or another kind of booby trap?

"Look," Hardaway said. "I know we might have gotten off on the wrong foot, but we can talk about this. Divide up the loot, and we can all walk away, nobody the wiser. What do you say?"

"I think you need to shut the fuck up," Fiona said. "And tell us how many more guys are out there."

"Two," Hardaway said.

I leaned closer, trying to discern the bags' contents based on the lumps straining against the canvas. Each bag had a giant 'X' in faded marker on its side, except for the one on the bottom, which had three. What did that mean? The Dean was playing mind-games from beyond the grave.

"We couldn't figure out who you were," Hardaway said, meaning me.

"That's a good question," I said, pulling more bricks away and setting them in a growing stack to my left.

"I meant your name," the cop said. "Spare me any existential bullshit."

"The existential bullshit is all you're going to get," I said, taking the edge of the handle and sliding it very carefully beneath the bottom duffel bag. The tip scraped stone. No wires or metal edges I could feel. "When I remember who I used to be, it's like a whole different person. How I dressed, how I thought, the decisions I made. Then I realize, I really *was* a different person. Every cell in my body's replaced itself by now. The beliefs I had at the time—well, those are just gone as if they never existed. And most of the people who remember me from back then, they're all dead."

Hardaway sighed. "You know what? Forget I fuckin' asked."

"To put it another way: I used to slaughter people for a living," I said. "Now I just maim them for life. But I'm trying to figure out a new act."

The cop turned to Fiona. "And how'd you fall in with this wacko?"

"He saved my life," Fiona said. "Then I made the mistake of shooting him in the back and leaving him for dead. But don't worry, we're all good now."

"You meet all types in this city," the cop said.

"No mine or anything beneath," I said, extracting the handle. Rising again, I gingerly lifted off the first duffel bag. It was absurdly heavy, sagging in my arms. I could only hope it was something good, like shrink-wrapped packs of hundred-dollar bills. But it could also be packs of C-4 primed to blow.

The radio spat static, followed by a voice boiling with

anger and panic: *"Whoever's in there, come out or we're killing this man. You have one minute."*

"It's showtime," I said. "You got a good plan?"

30

BILL TENSED AS Hardaway and Tattoo disappeared into the lighthouse. Soul Patch stood a little to his left, behind a tree, his pistol loose against his hip. Crew Cut lay on the muddy ground to Bill's right, peering through the thermal scope of the rifle.

An explosion from within the lighthouse. Soul Patch flinched, but Crew Cut remained perfectly still except for his finger tensing on the trigger.

"Sounded like a shotgun," Bill offered.

"Shut up," Crew Cut said. "I'm sure they're kicking someone's ass in there." But he rose to a crouch and moved a few more feet to his right, setting up a new position behind a low pile of rubble and weeds. Seeking a bit more cover.

Not so confident, are you? Bill thought, glad for how the night hid the smile tugging at his lips.

Soul Patch lifted his radio and murmured: "Hardaway? Report."

Silence from the radio. From inside the lighthouse, a muffled rustle. I bet my baby just pulled one of her world-famous ambushes, Bill thought. But who's the guy she's with? I didn't think we had any combat-ready friends left in New York.

Soul Patch tried again: "Hardaway? Damn it, answer."

Thumping from within the building. Like someone was pounding on bricks. No rhythm to it. Was someone signaling for help? Trying to tell him something?

Another burst of wind through the trees, the most powerful one in the past few minutes. From deeper in the forest behind them, what sounded like a large tree crashed into denser foliage, a symphony of breaking wood and whispering branches. How long until the hurricane roared back in? An hour? Less.

"Screw it," Crew Cut said. "Toss me that radio."

Soul Patch tossed it underhand to Crew Cut, who rolled onto his side to catch it in midair. Retaking his position behind his rifle, the older cop sighed and bent his head forward, his brow resting against the scope. As if readying himself for whatever might come next.

Hitting the radio's button, Crew Cut said: *"Whoever's in there, come out or we're killing this man. You have one minute."*

Bill tensed. It was almost funny, after all the events of the past hours, how he still had some adrenaline left in him. "Don't I get a say in it?" he said, trying to prod them a little, but it came out resigned, weak.

Crew Cut tossed the radio aside and bent his eye to the scope, his finger on the rifle's trigger. Soul Patch crouched, straight-arming his pistol beyond the tree trunk. Bill, realizing he was a little too exposed, knelt on one knee.

A man spoke from the doorway: "We have the money. And your partner."

Bill's breath caught in his throat. He remembered a burning barn, a man in an Elvis jumpsuit with a high-powered rifle in each hand. You never forget a man's voice after you've stood beside him and fired at wave after wave of rednecks intent on killing you. But Fiona had shot him in the back, killed him, right? And Fiona was always very good at confirming the kill.

"Partner?" Crew Cut yelled.

"The woman."

"What happened to the other one?"

"He lost his head."

Crew Cut bowed his head again, swallowed. "Why don't you send her and the money over here," he said, "and we'll send back your boy? Fair exchange."

"It's three bags. We're keeping two," the assassin said.

Crew Cut clicked his tongue. When Soul Patch looked over, he waved two fingers to the right—ordering him to flank.

"What say you," the assassin called, louder. "We have a deal?"

"We get two bags," Crew Cut shouted back. "You keep one. We got the firepower and way more people, son."

Bill considered his options. If Crew Cut threatened Fiona's life, he could flop on top of him. Even if he blew up, he'd take this prick with him. Hopefully Fiona wouldn't be standing too close—Bill really didn't like the idea of splattering her with his bits. *One for the road, honey!* What other options did he have?

"Fine," the assassin called. "We're sending her out."

Soul Patch left the cover of the tree and circled to the left, barely visible, and he must have seen something because he crouched a bit, extending his pistol, and Bill told himself he needed to shout, to warn the assassin before Soul Patch could fire—

A deeper shadow rose behind Soul Patch. Fiona's arm wrapped around the cop's neck, a pistol pressed against his temple. "Hello," Fiona told him.

Crew Cut was incredibly fast. Bill heard a click he later realized was the man's knees cracking as he stood from behind the rifle, but before Bill could pivot, the older cop was behind him, forearm locking across his throat, breath loud in his ear. Crew Cut had his pistol out and jammed hard into the thin bone of Bill's temple.

And from the doorway stepped Hardaway, a bulging duffel bag in each hand. A stubby shotgun to the back of her neck, a pale hand gripping her shoulder, a sliver of a familiar face: the assassin, his cheeks a little paunchier, his hair much more of a mess. At least he wasn't wearing an idiotic rhinestone jumpsuit. Despite the weight of the bags and the shotgun to the back of her head, Hardaway's face was a blank mask, and Bill almost admired her. She was an ice queen, a tough lady.

"Bill," the assassin said. "Looking good, man."

"You fucker," Crew Cut said. "Who are you?"

"Nobody," the assassin said, poking Hardaway with the shotgun. She stopped. They were maybe five feet away from the door, more than twenty feet from anyone else. "Also a nobody who happens to find himself in a three-way hostage situation in the middle of a hurricane. Anyone want to acknowledge how weird this is? How's it going, Bill?"

"I've had better nights," Bill said, his throat working painfully against Crew Cut's forearm. "What you been up to?"

The assassin shrugged. "Oh, you know, recovering from gunshot wounds, that kind of stuff."

Bill could sense Crew Cut's confusion. He let his cuffed hands drift to his left, close to Crew Cut's hip pocket. "You still killing people for money?" he asked.

"I was breaking folks' arms for a hot minute, but that was more of a side gig. Now I'm thinking of something else." The assassin glanced to his right, toward Fiona and Soul Patch.

"I've been thinking of a career change myself," Bill said. "The hustle's getting old." Bill's fingers skimmed the edge of Crew Cut's pants pocket, but the cuffs made it difficult to maneuver. The cuff-chain clinking a little too much. He let his hands drop away, frustrated. Try again in a second.

"I was thinking of becoming a writer, actually," the assassin said. "Did you know you can make a fortune off romance novels? I was thinking of specializing in hockey romance, there's a buck there. Lots of bored hockey moms."

"What the fuck?" Crew Cut asked.

The assassin's voice rose into the sonorous tones of an audiobook narrator: "'Her sex was as smooth as if the Zamboni had just done three passes, and as my hard puck slid into the net, the sirens in my head started sounding and my ears filled with the elated screams of a single member of the crowd.'"

"Maybe you should go back to killing people," Fiona called. "Stick with your strengths."

"Let's get this the fuck over with," Crew Cut said.

"Fine," the assassin said. "Send Bill over here."

"No. No way. You send my boy over to me," Crew Cut said, jutting his chin at Soul Patch. "Once he's over here, you send our lady, and we send Bill at the same time. Deal?"

The assassin glanced at Fiona, who nodded. Shoving Soul

Patch at Crew Cut, she backed toward the trees, her pistol aimed at the departing man's spine. Soul Patch stumbled across the clearing toward Crew Cut like a prisoner freed from a prison camp, his knees loose. When he closed to within a yard, his left foot rammed into a loose root. Bill raised his hands to prevent the man from ramming into him just as Crew Cut leaned forward, trying to use Bill as a shield against Soul Patch's momentum. Soul Patch bumped off Bill's shoulder before falling to his knees.

"Get your shit together," Crew Cut snapped, readjusting his arm on Bill's throat.

"Sorry," Soul Patch said, rising again.

"Now Hardaway comes over here," Crew Cut said, dropping his arm from Bill's throat and taking a step back. "And this guy walks to you. Step for step, understand?"

"Right," the assassin said.

"We're almost home, baby," Fiona called.

Crew Cut dropped something in Bill's pocket, heavy but small. "That's the key to the explosive around your neck," he said. "Once you get over there—and only when you get over there—can you unlock it. Understood?"

"Sure," Bill said, and took one step away from Crew Cut. Then another.

On the far side of the weedy field, Hardaway mirrored his movements, her forearms straining under the weight of the bags.

Bill took another three steps.

"There are markings on the bags," Hardaway said through clenched teeth. "Someone drew an X on one, three on the other."

"What's that mean, Bill?" Crew Cut asked.

"The one with the single X, it has an explosive device in

it. You pull the zipper, it'll blow. The other one, it's clean." Bill took another step forward, the base of his neck itching. That's where he'll shoot me, he thought.

"How can I believe that?" Crew Cut asked.

"The Dean thought three was his lucky number. He was almost psychotic about it," Bill said, taking another step. "If it's a one, it's got the claymore inside."

"Well, we'll see," Crew Cut said. "Keep going."

Bill took ten more steps, until he and Hardaway were abreast of one another. The cop's eyes blazing a hole through his head. Under different circumstances, he might have winked or smirked at her, but not tonight, not after everything they'd been though. He just wanted to go home.

Then Hardaway slipped past him. This was the dangerous part now. Everyone was close enough to their respective home bases to feel safer about shooting, and he still had this explosive around his neck. He glanced to his left, but Fiona was already gone. Was she flanking them again? Good tactics, but he didn't want to do anything to make Crew Cut excitable.

"Welcome," the assassin said, retreating to the doorway ahead of Bill. "If they're stupid enough to fire, I want you to hit the ground and crawl, got it?"

"I have so many questions for you," Bill said, turning to regard the cops.

Hardaway reached Crew Cut and, with a sigh, gently lowered the duffel bags. Soul Patch stood a little to their right, scanning for Fiona, his face hard with anger now. He wasn't the real problem, though, because Fiona could blast him from pretty much any distance. No, Crew Cut was about to become the real problem—a genuinely warm smile split his rocky face.

"Bill," Crew Cut said, sweet and thick as maple syrup.

At his feet, Hardaway bent down and fiddled with the zipper of the duffel bag marked with the triple X. "You know he's lying, right? If he told us this one's booby-trapped, then it's got to be the other one. He's trying to kill us."

"I swear, I'm not lying," Bill said. "The Dean was a paranoid guy."

"It doesn't matter," Crew Cut said, his hand dipping into his pocket. "Because you're going straight to Hell."

The assassin began to lift the shotgun, but Bill placed a hand on the barrels, stopping him in mid-swing. Bill shot a look at the trees, hoping Fiona picked up on his signal: Don't do anything.

Crew Cut scrambled in his pockets, his face blank with confusion.

"Oh," Bill said, holding up the fob. "Looking for this?"

Crew Cut's eyes widened.

"I pickpocketed you when that chump bumped into us," Bill said. "Sorry."

Hardaway gripped the zipper and pulled.

Crew Cut raised his pistol. "Motherf—"

At his feet, Hardaway gasped: "There's a—"

Bill hurled himself backwards into the assassin, knocking them through the doorway into the lighthouse's front room. A concussive boom slammed pain into his eardrums. He spat dust and pebbles, the assassin yelling something in his face impossible to figure out over the ringing in his ears—

He sat up. The assassin was already on his feet, scrambling low out of the doorway toward the clearing, where Crew Cut had been reduced to a pair of boots standing beside a smoking crater. It was raining again, no, hailing—little bits tinkling musically on the stone step between his feet.

No, not hail. Teeth.

Bits of red splattered the weeds. Then bigger chunks crackled branches in the woods beyond. It was raining cops. The Dean's parting gift.

A pale flash at the edge of the clearing. Soul Patch stumbled upright, his head a bloody mess. The ringing in Bill's ears was already beginning to clear, allowing him to hear the man's last words as he shouted:

"What smoke you crackin'!"

A flash from the trees, and Soul Patch's head exploded.

Fiona trotted through the grass, the smoking gun in her hand, to wrap her arms around Bill's waist, sink her face against his chest. She was smiling but also sniffling like she was about to cry.

He wove a dusty, bloody hand through her hair. "Hey, sweetie."

"Hey yourself," she said.

"Thank you for coming for me."

She laughed against his throat. "How'd you know which bag was booby-trapped?"

"The Dean was a paranoid fuck. I figured they were all booby-trapped. And I was right." He tapped the collar around his neck. "Hold on, let me get this fucking thing off me."

31

THE STORM PASSED.

The rain stopped first, the last few drops squeezed from a bruised sky brightening in the east. The wind powered for another hour before winding down into exhausted puffs. They watched its dying from their refuge in an office on Oak Point Avenue, which fronted the bay.

Wonder of wonders, the boat Bill spotted in the brush along the island's northern shore had an outboard motor. They had roared for the Bronx shore as the eyewall approached, bucking and bouncing across the swells so hard Fiona was convinced they would flip and drown within sight of shore—if the duffel bag nestled in the boat's bow didn't explode first. But they made it, scrambling over the concrete blocks separating the avenue from the water, then splashing across the parking lot to the first door in the first building they saw: a shipping office.

The assassin used the shotgun to blow off the lock. They sprinted inside, jamming a chair against the broken door and retreating to the windowless kitchen. The power was out, preventing them from using the microwave, but they gorged themselves on energy bars and snacks they found in the cabinets while they ransacked the closets for anything useful.

They found dry workmen's clothes in the largest supply closet: t-shirts and fleeces with the shipping company's bright logo, along with neatly cleaned and pressed coveralls. After changing, they moved to the front office, too exhausted to say anything to each other or do anything except sit on the desks and eat and stare out the windows as the hurricane subjected the city to a second pummeling, the glass flickering with lightning. The wind slammed against the broken door, trying to get in, but the chair held.

"This is maybe the understatement of the century," Bill told the assassin, "But I'm surprised you're here."

"I have a way of turning up when I'm needed," the assassin said.

"I still don't know your name."

The assassin shrugged. "I was born a John, but I never felt like a John, you know?"

After dawn, when it was light enough in the office to see properly, Bill found a pair of sharp scissors in a drawer. Feeling the bottom of the duffel bag, he punched the tips of the scissors through the canvas and began to cut a straight line.

He stopped after a second so Fiona could shine a flashlight through the gap.

No wires.

He kept cutting.

"When did you become an explosives expert?" the assassin asked.

"I saw 'The Hurt Locker' at least twice," Bill said, snipping a wider gap.

In slow motion, he reached in and pulled out the bag's contents onto the desk: a couple hundred thousand dollars in plastic-wrapped stacks of fifty-dollar bills, a sack of gold and silver jewelry, and a waterproof bag with three brightly colored hard drives cocooned in bubble wrap.

"What do you think?" Bill asked, holding up the hard drives. "Crypto? Blackmail images? Some combination of all of the above?"

"I'd bet on crypto. The Dean never stopped talking about Bitcoin near the end of his life," the assassin said. "All the more reason he deserved to die, frankly."

"Well, it's either worth a billion or a couple of cents, depending on the day," Bill slid two of the hard drives over to the assassin. "What do you say, you keep two, we keep one? Luck of the draw?"

"Sure." The assassin slid the drives into the large hip pocket of the coveralls. "But if it's just images of the mayor having sexual congress with a goat, we're going to need to re-negotiate."

"I don't want to know why that was your first thought," Fiona said, and sighed. She wasn't cold any longer—the dry clothes had solved that part nicely—but her every bone and muscle throbbed. Tomorrow wouldn't be pretty. Neither would the day after, unless she stayed pleasantly drunk. How many more years could she keep doing this crap?

Too few.

Time to quit and do something else, maybe.

But what?

They would figure it out.

"We all have our kicks." The assassin nodded at the piles of cash. "What about those?"

"Even split?" Bill said, glancing at Fiona, who nodded.

"That's fine," Fiona said. "We'll need all of it. Head out of town until things cool down with that billionaire prick, if they ever do."

"Billionaire prick?" Bill asked, retrieving the flashlight from Fiona so he could stick it into the gap in the bag. The light found the metallic back of a claymore mine, wired crudely to the zipper. Bill shuddered and let the gap fall closed.

"My mission. This billionaire with a penthouse, Boz wanted me to steal a server." Fiona slapped her forehead, realizing Bill didn't know any of this. "I found a kid there, they were going to take her kidneys out and put them in this billionaire, so I saved her." She pointed at the assassin. "Then he saved me."

Bill nodded his thanks to the assassin. "What happened to the kid?"

"She's at our place, along with Fireball. I guess we'd have to make a decision about what to do with her." She found Bill's cold hand, squeezed it twice.

"I have an idea," the assassin said, pulling out his phone. "Remember that app?"

Fiona turned to Bill. "It's an app for criminals. You can bid on jobs."

Bill's eyebrows rose.

"While I still have a little bit of battery power, let's put a hit on ol' Beau." The assassin grinned. "Starting off at, say, half a million? Heck, if there's any crypto on these hard drives, I'll pay it out of there. Consider it my gift to you."

"Half a million unless he backs off?" Bill asked.

"Nah." The assassin flashed teeth. "Guys like him, they

never back off. We're just gonna request his head on a pike. Have them stick it on Fifth Avenue somewhere as a warning to others? Why not? You can order anything these days."

Fiona felt a chill. It's a good thing this guy is on our side, she thought. We wouldn't be alive otherwise.

"Done," the assassin said, tapping his screen twice before sliding the phone into his pocket. "What say we get some breakfast?"

"I'm not sure anywhere is open," Bill said.

"It's New York," Fiona said. "Someplace is always open."

Bill pulled a blank piece of paper from a nearby printer, wrote 'CALL BOMB SQUAD' on it in large letters, and left it beside the crumpled remains of the duffel bag. Stuffing the money and hard drives and other loot into a trash bag, he kicked the chair away from the door and marched into the light, Fiona and the assassin right behind him. The hurricane's last winds had battered down the chain-link fence separating the office building from the parking lot next door, revealing rows of cement-mixers and other construction vehicles. They wandered until they found a pickup maybe three decades old but in fine shape, except for a crack in the windshield.

"It's a stick-shift," Bill said, squinting through the driver's window. "Also known as the Millennial anti-theft device. I bet it doesn't have an alarm, either."

"I'll take that bet," the assassin said. "What you want to put down? A hundred thousand? Two?"

"How about breakfast?" Bill said.

"Fine," the assassin said.

"The first car I ever stole was a stick," Bill said, stooping to retrieve a chunk of brick from beside the front tire. "I sold it to a chop shop for enough to buy a PlayStation."

"You never told me that," Fiona said.

Bill smashed the brick into the window, cracking it. A second blow, and the shattered glass rained onto the driver's seat. "I got to keep some secrets," he said, unlocking the door and opening it. "Keeps the relationship fresh. I win, by the way."

"Fine," the assassin chuckled. "Go wild at breakfast. Order a second waffle."

"I could settle for a mimosa," Fiona said. "The more alcohol, the better."

Bill swept away the glass from the driver's seat before sliding into the truck. Opening the glove compartment, he sorted through the piles of papers and assorted tools until he unearthed a small screwdriver. Slotted the tip into the ignition slot and twisted. The motor roared to life.

"Didn't think it'd be that easy," he said, gesturing for them to climb in. "Just think, in a couple more years, there's no way you could hotwire anything. Some A.I. will come out of the dashboard and strangle you if you try to steal the car. Another one of my skills rendered obsolete."

Fiona climbed through the passenger side, followed by the assassin. It was a tight squeeze. Fiona placed her hand on Bill's thigh and squeezed as he shifted the truck into gear and bumped over the fallen fence, veering south toward hazy Manhattan in the distance. They drove in silence, and Fiona imagined they were all feeling what she always felt after a near-death experience: an awareness of the cool air slipping down their nostrils, warming in their throats, expanding their lungs and chests. The texture of fabric beneath their fingertips. The way your eye seemed hyper-sensitive to every detail, especially the extraordinary colors blooming above the city's skyscrapers, purple and orange over the palest shade of blue.

Bill had to detour around some flooded roads, but they progressed through Manhattan far faster than Fiona had any right to hope. New Yorkers were starting to emerge from shelter, most of them holding their phones aloft so they could record the destruction. On 125th, an enterprising soul had set up a card table and was selling batteries, flashlights, and power tools at an absurd markup. They were far enough south to see something unusual: the ultra-thin needle of the Battery Park skyscraper where Fiona had started off the night's destruction, well, it looked like the tip of a burning match. The top floor was on fire, black smoke boiling into the bruised heavens.

"Looks like someone took you up on the bid," she told the assassin.

The assassin pulled out his phone, swiped through a screen, and chuckled. "Looks like every degenerate in the city turned out for that one."

"You know, we all did pretty good," Bill said. "Maybe we should make it a permanent thing, go into business together."

"Why not?" the assassin said. "I need something to do."

"We'd probably kill each other before the week is out," Fiona said. "But maybe not. Let's talk about it over pancakes."

NICK KOLAKOWSKI IS the Derringer- and Anthony-nominated author of Maxine Unleashes Doomsday and Boise Longpig Hunting Club, as well as the Love & Bullets trilogy of novellas. He lives and writes in New York City. Visit him virtually at nickkolakowski.com.